A DONATION OF MURDER
A SEABREEZE BOOKSHOP COZY MYSTERY BOOK 12

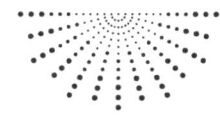

PENNY BROOKE

Copyright © 2024 by Penny Brooke

All rights reserved.

No part of this book may be reproduced in any form or by any electronic or mechanical means, including information storage and retrieval systems, without written permission from the author, except for the use of brief quotations in a book review.

This is a work of fiction. Names, places, characters, and incidents are either the product of the author's imagination or are used fictitiously, and any resemblance to any actual persons, living or dead, organizations, events or locales is entirely coincidental.

CHAPTER ONE

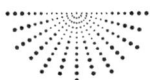

I pulled a long-sleeved tee out of a box of donations.

"Nice!" I whispered to myself. The shirt was blanket-soft, and the rich navy stripes were the perfect pop of color against the crisp white background.

Volunteering to sort items for the community-wide sale had its advantages—like getting first pick on the bargains. Since Somerset Harbor was a wealthy seaside enclave not far from Cape Cod, there could be some major finds in the shopping bags and boxes piled up against the wall of the Seabreeze Bookshop.

Then I checked the label, and, just as I expected, this was a real score. Never would I ever buy a full-price Yves Saint Laurent on a bookshop paycheck. Managing my gran's store was a job I adored—but not for monetary reasons. The bookshelves sent me on some exotic armchair travel. The memoirs let me peek into the way the rich and famous lived. But outside the pages? It was a bargain-hunting, coupon-cutting kind of life.

Not that I didn't treat myself every now and then. The Seabreeze was doing well, thanks to a robust online business and loyal customers in town. But being careful with my money had become a habit that I wanted to keep.

"I'm taking this," I said, holding up the shirt for my friend Elizabeth.

"What happened to your goal of clearing out that nice space in your closet?" she asked me with a laugh. "At least enough to pull a sweater off the shelf without some enormous pile of clothes falling into your face?"

She had seen my closet. And she, of course, was right. Which is why I'd packed up three boxes of my own for the sale, which would benefit the Somerset Harbor Youth Foundation.

"Since I cleared that space," I said, "there's room for this great shirt. Plus, it's all for a great cause." The proceeds would be used to send underprivileged students to the yearly summer camp held on our gorgeous beaches. The Seabreeze was one of four collection points in town.

"Hey, can you watch the store while I run to the dry cleaner's?" I asked Elizabeth.

"No worries. I'll be here," she said as she grabbed another box. After a busy morning, we seemed to have hit a lull, sending us to the back to sort.

Upon hearing "run"—one of his magic words—my golden retriever Gatsby leaped up from his nap. In a matter of just seconds, he could go from snoring to a great big blur of tail-wagging joy. He was always more than ready to visit all his friends in the downtown shops.

"Come on, boy. Let's go!" I said as I grabbed the leash. Then I got two dresses from the back of my car and set off across the street with Gatsby to the Clean and Bright dry cleaner's. The warm breeze carried with it the scent of the sea, and the door at the Clean and Bright was open to let in the sun and the near-perfect temps.

As I stepped inside the door, I was glad to see Lillian Clay behind the counter. Mostly, she stayed in the back and did alterations, but I always loved the chance to chat with her. Lillian was an avid reader, and the two of us had a kind of game we'd play when I saw her around town. On a whim, she'd come up with a list of themes and subjects to describe the perfect read for her current mood. And I'm proud to say I (nearly) always met the challenge of throwing out a title within minutes.

"How's it going, Lillian?" I handed her my dresses.

She gave me a smile. "I'd like to read a mystery about...I know! A poet!" She pondered for a moment. "And I'd really love a setting that would leave me all immersed in aristocratic privilege. Doesn't that sound fun?"

I tilted my head, running titles through my mind. "Have you read Kate Morton? *The House at Riverton!* Lillian, you'd adore it. And if you love her like I do, I can fix you up with more."

"Never heard of her, but you never steer me wrong." She added a tag to my red silk dress. "This is beautiful," she said.

That gave me a kind of thrill because Lillian, out of everyone in town, would be the one to know. In a past life she had worked for a major fashion house in New York before she moved to Massachusetts after her husband's death. It must have been a shock, going from the design studios of the exclusive and much-heralded Pierre Blanchet to the small but well-lit alterations room at the Clean and Bright. But she had New England roots, and at fifty-four, she had begun to long for less traffic and more trees. Mostly, she had wanted to interact with people who had time to really listen to the answer when they asked about your day.

"I'll try to get by the store today and grab that book," she said, handing a dog treat to Gatsby from a jar on the counter. "Something for a good boy," she cooed.

Gatsby barked his thanks before he eagerly took the treat from her outstretched hand.

"I'll have some time for reading on the plane next week," she told me as a smile spread across her cheeks. "Oh, Rue, I'm off to France! My sister's going too."

"Oh, Lillian, that's amazing." William from the Clean and Bright had been trying for a while to get her to take the vacation days that she was due. But after her fast-paced life in New York, she had seemed content to enjoy the simple pleasures of a stroll on the beach or a lobster roll at Asher's Bistro down the street.

Now, a childlike joy shone in her green eyes. "The first stop is—you'll never guess. I've booked us on a tour of those gorgeous castles—the Château de Chambord, the Château de Chenonceau—in the Loire Valley." She let out a sigh. "It just does not seem real."

I understood at once how much this trip would mean. When you were in the business of listening carefully to customers to curate their reading lists, you were entrusted with the privilege of looking deep inside them; you got to see their dreams. To Lillian, I had sold a lot of books in which the plots unfolded on sweeping, grand estates. Other books were set in medieval castles with hidden rooms and secrets. And she loved children's books as well, in which feisty princesses did battle against dragons—or maybe evil kings—to save their kingdoms by the sea.

The bell on the door signaled the arrival of another customer, and her expression quickly changed. She held her hand to her chest, as if she was startled by the bell she must hear all day long.

"Are you okay?" I asked.

"Oh, thank you, Rue. I'm fine." She took a deep breath. "I just woke up tired today. A head cold, I believe." She smiled at the man who had entered, a bag of clothes in his arms.

"Well, rest up for your trip." I held my hand up in goodbye. "Come by for that book, and I'll set aside some others. That's a long time on the plane."

I crossed the oak-lined street and passed The Cupcakery, where the sugary aromas blended with the salty scent of sea carried by the wind.

The owner was outside, placing a sign on the door about the rummage sale. "Come on in!" he boomed. His smile reached the tip of his elaborate mustache, and his bright purple apron strained against his hefty girth. "I just made a fresh batch of German chocolate cupcakes.

The Flavor of the Day! With coconut frosting and pecans."

"Okay, that sounds amazing, but please don't tempt me, Ned."

My furry friend, however, didn't share my worry over calories and sugar. The eager dog, in fact, was halfway to the counter, where Ned kept a stash of Pup Cakes, freshly made each morning and free to his canine pals.

"He's being spoiled today," I told Ned with a smile. "We've already been to the Clean and Bright, where he got a treat from Lillian."

"Ah, yes, Lillian Clay! Who works magic with her needle. What a lucky happenstance to have her across the street." Ned laughed and touched his belly. "All this sampling of cupcakes is always sending me to her so she can let out some seams, make my shirts more roomy." He spread his arms out in a shrug. "But what is a guy to do? All day long it is my job to mix and stir and bake. And, of course, to taste."

"And you do it well." I studied the offerings in the glass case, trying to decide whether to give in to a maple-bacon cupcake or one of Ned's signature key-lime-pie-flavored beauties. Made with his grandmother's recipe, the key-lime ones had been voted Best Sweet Treat in New England three years in a row. That was great for all of us, sending droves of cupcake-loving tourists into the downtown shops.

"Give me a key lime," I said.

"My grandma's pride and joy!" Ned beamed, but in his eyes, I saw a weariness, unusual for the spirited cupcake baker.

Behind him was a youthful portrait of his grandmother Kate, whose perfect blend of ingredients helped merchants breathe more easily when the off seasons hit. Her long curls were held back in a loose ponytail and, with a hint of mischief in her eyes, she looked like she could tell a good joke as well as bake an awesome cupcake.

I handed Ned my Visa and watched him with concern. "You look tired," I said.

"Been handling the counter by myself today with so many people sick," he said. "And tomorrow the same story."

"I know how that can be," I said with a sympathetic smile. Owning a business could be rough, and the town in recent weeks had been hit hard by the flu. Thankfully, the bookstore staff had managed to stay well.

"On second thought," I said, "add another cupcake to my order, please. Elizabeth would love me if I brought her back one of those peanut-butter ones she likes." I watched as he retrieved Elizabeth's favorite cupcake, which was decorated with mini chocolate cookies in the shape of hearts. "Hey, did you hear the news?" I asked. "Lillian's off to France!"

"When?" I could have sworn he looked alarmed before the trademark smile returned.

"I think she said next week."

"Oh, yeah? I hadn't heard," he said, breathing hard while he handed me my treats in the trademark bright box. "Hey, I've left a small bag by the door with some donations, Rue. Would you mind grabbing that on your way out the door? My wife's been clearing space, and she's started with the kitchen." Then something outside caught his eye. "Hey, get in here, John!" he called to a passerby. "Did you hear that Lillian Clay is going on a grand tour of France? I think that calls for a cupcake."

"Doesn't everything?" I asked him with a laugh. He was almost as good at sales as he was at baking. Even the smallest bits of daily joy should be celebrated with a gaily decorated sugary confection, according to the philosophy of Somerset Harbor's favorite baker.

The elderly owner of Soups and Sauces Café popped his head into the door. "She must be so excited—France!" he said with a smile. "Hey, Ned, did you happen to make a batch of the vanilla ones today? The ones with the chocolate chips?"

"You bet I did," said Ned.

Gatsby greeted John with a lick of his hand, and I waved goodbye to the men. As I stepped out onto the sidewalk, the breeze had disappeared, and gray clouds had moved in to blot out the sun. Despite Lillian's news and the treats inside my box, I was feeling anxious. Something just seemed off that day.

It was something about the way Lillian had been jumpy when the bell had jingled to signal an arrival. And in the way that Ned's ever-present smile hadn't reached his eyes. I tried to ignore the feeling, but I also knew how often my instincts were correct in a town that had seen more than its share of heartbreak.

Still, nothing could have prepared me for the news that swept through town in the late afternoon two days after that. I was packing shipments for online customers when I saw Elizabeth speaking to some women. Her eyes were clouded over, her hand pressed to her chest. The group was talking quietly near the biographies, and I watched as one of them dabbed away a tear.

Then Elizabeth made her way to me, and her face was white. "Oh Rue, you won't believe it," she said softly. "It's…oh, it's Lillian Clay." Tears sprung to her eyes as she told me the news. "They just found her—dead."

"What?" I gasped. "What happened?"

Elizabeth's voice was trembling. "It's just horrific,

Rue. Someone jabbed a pair of fabric scissors into her wrist and neck."

We stood in a stunned silence. Those awful words I'd heard come out of my friend's mouth—no way could they be right. "Do they know who?" I asked. "Or why?"

Elizabeth shook her head, and I sunk into a nearby reading chair. I hadn't been there long when I felt a tickling at my ankle and a cold nose on my cheek. Then I had a white cat and a gray one snuggled in my lap.

"Hello, Beasley. Hello, Ollie." I leaned back and closed my eyes, thankful for these friends, who somehow understood I needed their soft fur against me to still my pounding heart.

CHAPTER TWO

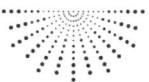

Murder by sewing scissors was a thing the local cops had heard of, although it was pretty rare.

"Those kind of scissors that she kept in her office have a wicked tip," explained my buddy Andy. "They're not like the ones that you and I are used to using." He'd stepped away from the police force to work in private investigations, but the chief still called him in to help on bigger cases. Now he had settled in on the big front porch of my gran's house, where I now resided while she was traveling the world. It was the end of a long day that had left Somerset Harbor shaken to its core.

"Who would do that, Andy? *Why?*" I asked. That was the refrain I had heard all day.

He took a sip of whiskey. "Robbery perhaps? But we

don't think so, Rue. They left the cash drawer undisturbed. And the only thing we've determined to be missing is a necklace Lillian had on earlier today, according to her boss. It wasn't on the body."

They'd killed her for *a necklace?* That did not sound right to me. I reached for the bottle next to me and refilled my cabernet. "Was it an expensive necklace?"

"No way of knowing at this point. William from the Clean and Bright said he believed the thing was silver, that it was a silver chain with three charms dangling off it. There was a little owl charm, he said, and blue stones for the eyes. There also was a star. And he believed the other charm was some kind of curved-shaped thing—a crescent moon perhaps."

"Interesting," I said. Lillian never had been a big fan of jewelry. She, who had once been in the business of creating haute couture, had simple tastes herself.

Her purse, Andy said, had been found behind her desk with three credit cards inside and almost forty bucks.

The look in Andy's eyes was the look he got at the end of his worst cases, not the start.

"You okay?" I asked.

He let out a sigh. "Sometimes the job is hard. She was a good woman, that Lillian—and people can be scum."

A sympathetic Gatsby let out a little whine. He

moved closer to his buddy Andy and set his head on his feet.

The day's atrocity had hit Andy hard enough that he'd let go of his normal stinginess with details about police investigations. He seemed to feel the need to talk, making sure I knew that anything he said was between the two of us. He had let me know, for instance, that Lillian had been the sole employee at the store for most of the day. The owner of the business had been occupied with a family move, and two of the employees had called in with the flu.

The police had followed up on records that gave the names and contact information of those customers who had picked up or dropped off their dry cleaning after Lillian was last seen by the owner, William Knolls. But no records could be found of any patrons of the business who'd come in for alterations as opposed to cleaning.

"Lillian kept a calendar with her appointments marked, but there were no names," said Andy. "There were just notations: 'Pants hemmed' or 'Bridesmaid's Dress.' You know, that kind of thing."

In addition to the dry-cleaning customers who had been interviewed, a couple of people had come forward to tell police that they'd seen Lillian on that day for

A DONATION OF MURDER

alterations. But that accounted for only two of the five appointments she had written down.

She was last seen alive at about ten o'clock.

I took a sip of wine. "Does William have a clue about who might have wanted to hurt Lillian?" I asked Andy.

"The whole thing is baffling." Andy scratched his ear. "Everyone loved Lillian."

Well, not everyone.

"So none of the people that you talked to knew of something different going on with her? That could maybe be a hint?" I asked.

"We've got nothing," Andy said.

That was just because the cops hadn't spent an afternoon at Reba's House of Beauty, where I happened to pop in the next day for a cut and highlights. It was a slow day at Reba's, and I was alone with Tiffany, my stylist, as familiar nineties tunes played softly in the background.

Alanis Morissette on the speakers seemed to capture the dark mood both of us were in as Tiffany Cantrell settled me into her chair. Lillian through the years had taken on a mentor role with the twenty-something-year-old stylist, who had a degree in fashion and dreamed of the New York fashion world Lillian had once conquered. Today she looked the part. The pink highlights in her hair were the only color in her look as she moved about in a short black dress, textured tights, and some great black boots.

"Lillian was just in here the day before it happened." Tiffany's face was white as she put a lightening solution on a long strand of my hair. "And she was just...*different*, Rue."

"Different how?" I asked.

"Well, first of all, she rushed in almost fifteen minutes late, which was not like her. You would not believe it, but Miss Organized herself had just about *forgotten* she was supposed to come in for me to do her hair. Which was the first weird thing." Tiffany pursed her lips. "And then I had to run out after her when I was finished with the cut and color. To give her back her purse—which she left sitting on the counter, plain as that water bottle." With her gaze, she directed my eyes to the cluttered counter with the bright orange water bottle that sat amid a jumble of shampoos and styling products.

Tiffany studied my hair, then moved to work on my right side. "And we're not talking just a trim," she told me. "This was for a major change in style—much shorter than she'd ever let me cut it. And she'd finally agreed that I could touch up the gray." Her eyes met mine in the mirror. "I was so excited," she continued. "I'd been telling her for years I could take ten years off her age with a little snip, a little color. And when she finally says yes, she...almost forgets to come?"

"Sounds like she was majorly stressed," I said.

Even though she had seemed okay—had seemed excited even—when I'd picked up my dress. "Did she say what was up?"

"You know how private Lillian was," Tiffany replied with a shrug as she separated out another strand of hair. "She did admit to me she was going through 'some stuff.' That was how she put it. And her whole vibe was different. She was all introspective, which was so not her." Tiffany stopped her work and frowned. "Right before she left, she made me promise her that I would always... how exactly did she put it? She made me promise I would always 'honor other people's joy.' What does that *even mean?* She never talked like that." Tiffany scrunched up her brow as she added more of the lightener to my hair. "I tried to ask her more about it, but then she changed the subject to the last two singers on *The Voice* and who did I think was best."

Hmm. If anybody knew what had been up with Lillian, Tiffany would be the one. Tiffany's mother had passed away when she was a child, and Lillian, to her regret, had never been able to have children. That helped to explain why the two of them had felt drawn to one another right away: the young girl without a mother, the mom without a child. It was almost just too perfect since Tiffany was obsessed with finding some of Lillian's rarefied success in the world of fashion. Hopefully one day in New York, but any job in fashion would do at the moment. Unfortunately, so far, her résumé had drawn no takers. But in the meantime, there were manicures and blowouts and updos to pay the bills.

A silence fell over the salon as she continued with my highlights. My mind went into overdrive as I thought about what Tiffany had said. That advice from Lillian—about doing right by people—almost had the ring of parting words of wisdom from a mentor to her mentee. Not just the kind of idle chitchat that passes between friends on a cut-and-color day.

I made a list in my mind of the things we knew about Lillian's life in the weeks before her murder.

She'd agreed to a new look after years of being stubborn about sticking to a style that was "not a bother." Her job, she always said, was to make others shine. All she wanted for herself was "easy:" clothes she could bend and work in, shoes that felt good on her feet, and no-fuss kind of hair.

We also knew that she'd bought tickets to leave the

country after years of never even taking off a few days to drive into Boston or visit family in Rhode Island.

I remembered how she'd startled the last time I saw her when the bell signaled a new guest at the Clean and Bright.

Had Lillian, in fact, been planning to get out of here, to get away from someone?

New hairstyle, renewed passport, brand-new life?

Or was I simply doing what Andy said I always did: turning the stuff of the real world into the kind of drama I read about in books? Real life didn't teem with the deep, dark secrets I read about in thrillers, he always joked to me. There were simpler explanations for most crimes, he said, such as greed or drugs.

Tiffany's voice jolted me out of my thoughts. Apparently, she also had been mulling over Lillian's final days.

"It was pretty clear," she said, "that Lillian didn't want to talk about what had her all freaked out. But under the dryer sometimes, people mumble to themselves. Under there is where you have some good thinking time—when you're all relaxed with that warm air blowing at you. Some people even sleep."

My heartbeat quickened just a little. "What did Lillian say?" I asked.

Tiffany put her hand on her hips as she thought back to that day. "It seems like she said something about a *travesty,* how she *could not believe it.* And I think she might have mumbled something...about a *garish color?*" She tilted her head and frowned. "That *garish-color* thing would have freaked me out except for the fact that the color I was giving her was nothing that I picked. Just what the good Lord gave her! I just covered up the gray to match the color she was born with."

I mulled over Lillian's words for the rest of my appointment. When Tiffany was done, I looked at myself in the mirror as the stylist unfastened and whipped off my protective smock. Tiffany, as usual, had done an awesome job, but my new soft waves with their reddish highlights gave me little joy. I was simply numb.

"Looking good!" said Tiffany as she nodded toward a box beside the register. "Could you take that when you go? It's stuff I pulled together for the Foundation sale, and hopefully I'll come up with some more next week. Still sorting through the closet."

"Thank you," I told her. Then something on the counter caught my eye: the familiar pink box that signaled something good inside from The Cupcakery. Through the clear plastic top, I could spy the bright green candy daisies that always decorated the Oreo cupcakes. And the pink icing next to it meant a strawberry-flavored cupcake or a pink lemonade.

I understood the sadness I was feeling could not be

cured by sugar, but my mouth had begun to water. When things were going wrong, I always looked to sweets and books for comfort.

"Oh, take a cupcake—please." Tiffany gave me a weak smile when she saw where I was looking. Then her eyes grew wet with tears.

"What's wrong?" I asked her softly.

"Lillian," she said in a whisper. "Lillian brought them in as a little treat. She came back about an hour after her weird appointment, and she brought us these."

After a moment of silence, we each took a cupcake. I touched mine to hers in a toast to our friend. Then the flavors of sweet and tart and tears blended on my tongue as the music of Nirvana wafted over us.

The rest of the day went by in a flash and a blur of customers. Big news had a way of bringing locals into the downtown shops to commiserate, trade theories with each other, and catch up on the latest news.

I was straightening some books on the nonfiction shelves when I heard a familiar voice. "Rue! Can you believe it?" Betsy Lawrence adjusted her purse on her arm. "I've just felt sick all day."

I gave her a hug. "It's like we're in a nightmare," I told her. "I keep hoping I'll wake up."

Betsy and I had become close friends over our common love of thrillers, which we dissected over nachos and Greek salads at Asher's across the street. A longtime district court judge, Betsy had an office in the courthouse just one block from the store. She was a fast reader and came in quite a lot.

Now, she brushed a stray blonde tendril from her eyes and frowned. "What do you have on these shelves to get me through the night? We've all had a rough week. Bring on the books and wine!"

"Bring on the wine! Bring on the wine!" squawked a loud voice behind us. It was the bookstore parrot, Zeke.

After a startled silence, there was nervous laughter in the aisles.

"Ah. Escape through a good book!" I said to Betsy. "You've come to the right place." I led her to the new releases, where I put into her hands the latest Louise Penny. "I devoured this one in two days," I said. "Lunch next week at Asher's? So we can discuss?"

"Absolutely," she told me. "Oh, and by the way, I dropped off a box at your office door. You know, for the sale."

"It's shaping up to be a good one. We appreciate it. Thanks!"

By that point, a young girl was waiting patiently to ask me a question, so Betsy kissed me on the cheek to say goodbye. "I'll continue browsing, and I'll see you next week," she said.

At the end of the day, I pulled off my heels and sank into a big chair in the Book Nook, the cozy spot where readers could relax with their selections. The store had finally grown quiet fifteen minutes before closing.

Elizabeth sat down next to me and sighed. "Who would have thought a murder would bring in a crowd?" she said. "I don't remember when we've been so busy when it's not the height of the tourist season."

"Everybody's horrified, and no one wants to be alone," I said. "Plus, some of them also came in to drop off their bags and boxes." New donations for the sale had accumulated as the day wore on.

Then I had an idea. "I want to check out Betsy's box!" I said, standing up. It would be a distraction, and I could almost bet she'd brought in some good stuff. Even though her clothes were often covered by a robe, Betsy had great style—and she was about my size.

"I can stay tonight if you want to sort donations for an hour or two," said Elizabeth. "We can order in a pizza."

"Works for me," I said. I followed Elizabeth to the back room, where we had donations sorted on a long work table. On the way, I grabbed Betsy's box, which I remembered had the logo of a printing company in town.

I cut into that one right away. On the very top was a small green pouch, heavy with jewelry. Score! This could be really good. First, I pulled out a chunky bracelet with blue and green glass beads.

"That one's really nice," cooed Elizabeth. "Why is she getting rid of that?"

I put it on my arm and held it up to the light.

Elizabeth let out a chuckle. "Mark my words," she said. "You will have more stuff at the end of this sale than before your so-called purge."

"Maybe so." I smiled. "But it's all for charity!"

Next, I pulled out a dainty silver chain with three tiny charms hanging off a topaz stone. There was a crescent moon, a star, and an owl with sapphire eyes.

Like the necklace Lillian had been wearing that was missing from the body.

I almost lost my breath.

"That one I really like," cooed Elizabeth, reaching out to touch the chain. "Maybe I'll buy this one if you decide to pass."

"I need to sit," I said, pulling out a chair as a ball of sickness rose up in my belly.

CHAPTER THREE

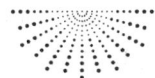

"This is huge," said Andy as he rubbed his hand across the top of his head. "Quite the clue you've found." The necklace lay before us on my office desk.

I'd called Andy right away after I explained to Elizabeth what was going on.

"We'll check this for fingerprints," he said, running through the steps in his mind. "We'll get William to the station right away to confirm this is the one. And, of course, we'll talk to Betsy. We'll check her schedule at the courthouse between the time that Lillian was last seen and the discovery of the body." He let out a sigh. "I guess there's good news here—we might just solve this thing! But I have to tell you, Rue: I'm floored by what you've found."

"This is unbelievable," I said. There had never been a hint of a scandal surrounding Betsy's time as a local judge. And she lived a rather quiet life when she was not at work: cultivating roses in her yard, reading thrillers, and volunteering at a local center where single mothers could get help with food and jobs. Had she and Lillian even been acquainted? I had no idea.

I sank down in my desk chair. "So, what happens next with Betsy? Will you let her know that you have the necklace?"

"That's up to the chief, of course." A crease formed on Andy's brow as he reached down to pet Gatsby. "If it were up to me, I might hold off at first with that information. And see what she will tell us. Once she knows what we found, she might shut up real quick."

My head was still spinning, and I shut my eyes, taking a deep breath. "I can't believe it, Andy."

He moved closer to me and put a warm hand on my shoulder. "Let's not jump to conclusions," he said to me gently. "Evidence like this always tells a story, but sometimes the story, Rue, is not what you assume. Just as an example, some people from the courthouse could have gone in together to pack up their donations. Maybe someone else there threw the necklace in the box."

"Or the killer could have dropped it! And Betsy

could have found it on the sidewalk and just picked it up," I said.

"And if it was not her style," said Andy, "she might have thrown it in the box to benefit the sale."

"Any other news?" I asked, and Andy sighed. It was a kind of dance we did when he was on a case in which I had an interest.

"Rue, you already know I can't talk about this stuff," he said.

Hmm. I eyed the necklace. "Well, at least one of us isn't stingy about sharing information." I gave him a wink. "And I might know more."

Andy raised a brow.

"I talked to Tiffany Cantrell today at Reba's House of Beauty," I began.

Andy listened carefully as I described the things that Lillian had mumbled to herself underneath the dryer. I updated him as well about the forgetfulness and the introspective mood that was so unusual for her.

"One of our detectives, Pete, talked to Ms. Cantrell as well." Andy brought his fingertips together in a V. "I believe he also made a note that Lillian didn't seem herself. But your report is much more detailed. That could be very helpful, Rue."

"Well, when you just ask a question like the cops are always doing, you get one kind of answer," I explained.

"But the answer…well, *expands* when you sit for a long while in a stylist's chair and let the conversation wander where it may."

He gave me a small smile and ran his hand through his sparse hair. "There's only so much time a stylist can spend on an old head like this, so that approach would never work for the likes of me and Pete."

"Lillian was upset," I mused, "but there seemed to be something more." With the deep thoughts she pressed on Tiffany. With finally letting her young friend give her a new look. And with the seizing of the dream trip, I sensed some kind of change that had been at work in Lillian.

Andy crossed his arms. "I got that feeling too. The last time I saw her, I was at the Clean and Bright to get my fishing pants. And when I got them home, I felt something in the pocket. One of those portable fish finders! A really fancy one."

Andy was well-known as one of the most skillful (or perhaps the luckiest) of our local fishermen. He was also teased a lot about how little time he spent out on the water. The move to private investigations had been supposed to give him more control of his own schedule. As it turned out, however, Andy was so eager to help his troubled clients that he immersed himself in work—and the striped bass and the haddock were much safer for it.

"That was quite the pricey surprise that she left you," I said.

"Very generous," said Andy.

The big box of cupcakes, the fish finder—why the sudden urge for gifts?

"Have you found out more about who might have come into the dry cleaner's yesterday?" I asked. An appeal had gone out on the news asking citizens to call police if they had seen Lillian on the day of her death or the day before.

Word had also quickly spread through Somerset Harbor's most effective means of communication: the talk and texts and calls between The Seafood Shack and Pete's Hardware, between Juice It Up and An Elegant Bouquet, and on and on and on.

Andy pulled out a wooden chair to take a seat. "We're still missing statements from three of the unknown customers she had on the calendar for alterations yesterday." He rubbed his forehead, frowning. "It's not like they haven't heard that we need them to come forward. What is wrong with people, Rue?"

"Maybe they picked up their alterations on their way out of town?" I asked. "And they haven't heard?"

Maybe one of them, but surely not all three.

I watched Andy, worried. He seemed a lot more tired with this case, quicker to get angry. And a lot less careful about spilling details to a non-professional like me. At least that last part, I was glad for. Hopefully, the current bad strain of the flu was not about to get him. I myself was always extra cranky at the beginning of a cold or flu.

Wordlessly, I got up and walked to the tea cart, bringing back his favorite Three-Berry Tea. "You okay?" I asked.

He gave me a weak smile as he took a sip. "Some of them just hit you harder than the others."

Beasley appeared to nudge his nose against Andy's ankle, settling against his foot as if to say he was sorry.

I brushed some hair from my eyes. "So, besides the necklace, are there any leads?"

"Unfortunately, no. Although we've talked to quite a few who talked to her that day and the day before—at the hair salon, the Sandwich Stop, the bank."

"And the Cupcakery."

Andy looked alert. "She was at the bakery?" he asked.

"She dropped off some cupcakes for the staff at Reba's. I know they were from Ned's—because I saw the box."

"Interesting," said Andy. "I was there at Ned's just this afternoon. With all of the interviews I've done, I kind of had skipped lunch, and I thought a cupcake might just hit the spot." A crease formed on his forehead.

A DONATION OF MURDER

"I find it very odd that he never mentioned seeing Lillian."

It was possible that Ned had just assumed a brief encounter—selling her a box of cupcakes—would not be helpful to the cops.

Except that there were signs asking people to come forward if they'd seen her that day. They had been printed by the merchants guild and were taped up in every business—and that included Ned's.

Ned had also told me he'd be working by himself that day. So it had to have been Ned who served Lillian at the counter.

"Elizabeth and I are staying late to sort," I said, "and we're sending out for pizza. Want to stay and eat? If your lunch was a cupcake, you need to do a little better when it comes to dinner."

"It's very tempting, Rue, but I'm gonna need to update the chief and do some work tonight." He raised an eyebrow at me as he stood. "Because of a certain friend of mine with an eagle eye, the case has taken quite a turn."

After he had gone, Elizabeth and I were quiet as we went about our work, both of us still dazed by the appearance of the necklace.

"I'm almost scared to open up another one of these," my friend managed to joke as she cut into some tape on another box. "I guess you never really know someone until you've sorted through the stuff they want to give away."

We both laughed nervously.

I put a nice chip-and-dip dish in the housewares section and added some hardcovers to the corner with the books. Our main job was to cull out any items that were stained or ripped or otherwise not suitable for sale. But to help the set-up crew, we planned to group the stuff in categories when we packed it back up for transport.

I reached for the small bag I'd picked up at Ned's. All of it was kitchen stuff: a garlic press, a can opener, and a kitchen timer. Plus, there were several cookbooks. "These look kind of old," I said, studying the worn hardback covers. They made me think of the books my gran had used when she made her well-loved pies and the macaroni and cheese that was my favorite as a girl. I flipped through one of them, and some papers fluttered out.

"Oooh. It's recipes," I said. Some had been cut out from newspapers that had by then turned yellow. Others were handwritten on small cards and creased sheets of paper.

Elizabeth moved closer. This was the exact thing my best friend was obsessed with: little bits of people's past.

She was the proprietor of Antiquities by Elizabeth in the corner of the bookshop, and customers adored the old photographs, postcards, and ephemera she carefully curated for her space.

"Lobster Newberg. Yum." She picked up a faded card with "Recipes" and a picture of a bluebird printed at the top.

I picked up another card. This one was a little larger and on heavy stock. Its handwritten words were faded to the point that they were hard to read. "This one should be good," I said. "This one's from The Fish House."

The restaurant in nearby Yarmouth was still going strong after many decades. Elizabeth and I would occasionally treat ourselves to dinner there when we had occasion to celebrate or commiserate—and sometimes "just because."

I studied the card in my hand. "This recipe, I think, would be hard to follow." I squinted hard at it. In addition to the problem of the fading ink, the words were in disarray. Someone had crossed out ingredients and squeezed others in their place in the tiniest of letters. Notes were written sideways in the margins, filling every space.

"Bring eggs to room temperature," said one.

"Don't overmix the batter," said another.

I had to tilt my head to read. "Someone did some serious experimenting with this recipe," I said.

"A recipe for what?" asked Elizabeth.

I squinted at the top of the card and gasped.

"It's for Key Lime Cupcakes."

And it had been packed inside the cookbook by Ned's wife—maybe by mistake.

Both of us were silent.

"But Ned's grandmother, Kate—she was a nurse," I said. "She did not work for a restaurant." Her story had been told so many times that all of us in town had memorized the details. Kate Lansing had lovingly cared for soldiers on medical evacuation flights, and they had later sought her out, enjoying the sweet treats from her oven, including her now-famous key-lime cupcakes. It was a recipe she'd created lovingly in her kitchen.

It was a family recipe, handed down with pride.

Unless…

For the second time that day, I wondered if someone I thought I knew was someone altogether different.

And for the second time that day, I found it hard to breathe.

CHAPTER FOUR

I took a deep breath and shot a text to Andy: "Call me now. Important."

If the recipe *had been* stolen—if the legendary cupcake story was nothing but a lie—could that be related to the case?

I was thinking maybe.

Ned was being weirdly secretive about seeing Lillian the day before she died. And earlier that week, he had seemed alarmed when I mentioned to him that she was off to France. If only for brief moments on that day, I'd seen glimpses of a man who was preoccupied and edgy, not the beloved jolly owner of what he proclaimed to be the "Happiest Spot in Town."

Had he figured out the recipe was missing?

But what on earth could that have to do with Lillian?

The buzzing of my phone cut into my thoughts.

"I have to make this quick." Andy sounded breathless on the other end. "Busy, busy night."

"I found something else!" I said. "In one of the boxes! A recipe for cupcakes, and I'm pretty sure—"

"Let me stop you now," he said in a rush. "One day soon I'd love to hear about these special cupcakes. And you can even make me some. But for now, I need to run and—"

"Not just any cupcakes, Andy."

"Rue, I really—"

"It's for *the* cupcakes. From the Cupcakery."

He was quiet for a moment. "The famous key-lime cupcakes? You found a recipe for those?" he asked. "In a *box of donations?*"

"It was in some stuff that Ned's wife packed up. A mistake, I'm sure. Someone—maybe Ned or even his grandmother—had stuck it in a cookbook that his wife decided she would toss."

Ned, of course, would have long ago memorized the recipe after mixing up batch after batch of his signature cupcake. In some of the many feature stories on the business, reporters had speculated about how many of the cupcakes had come out of his ovens since 1993, when he had set up shop. How high would they reach if you stacked them in a tower? How far would they

A DONATION OF MURDER

stretch across the neat landscapes of downtown and our white sandy beaches?

Andy let out a low whistle. "That's quite the piece of paper you've discovered, Rue. Ned will be so relieved it fell into your hands before the thing got sold. Can you imagine even? Fascinating story! But I really need to go."

"Andy, wait! Don't go! This thing might be so much bigger than a lost recipe. Because right there on top of the recipe card, it says—"

"You can tell me later, Rue, about whatever super-special ingredient makes those cupcakes so amazing. But right now, I'm on my way to the chief, and I really need to go."

I let out a sigh. "Okay then. You can call me later, and I'll save the recipe."

"Save the recipe? But why? Just give it back to Ned."

"I thought *you* might want it. Since—"

"Me?" A silence followed that before he continued. "Rue, I'm not a baker. I'm an investigator—who is very pushed for time."

"And if you will listen for *a second,* you'll be an investigator with a possible new *clue.*"

"A clue?"

When he allowed me to explain, I made quick work of describing how the card was linked to The Fish House, not the Cupcakery. I told him how the numerous

39

additions and the many cross-outs on the card detailed the long process of tweaking and experimenting—until some unknown chef had at last baked the perfect cupcake.

"Very interesting," he said after a pause. "And despicable as well if that recipe was stolen." He let out a sigh. "But the *real* evil on my mind is what was done to Lillian. So, as I've been saying, I really need to go."

"Andy, don't you see? It all could be connected!"

He took some time to think. "It's a bit of a stretch—but worth looking into," he decided. "I do find it somewhat suspect that Ned didn't say a word about seeing Lillian the day before she died. Especially with the cops making it so clear we need people to come forward." Andy cleared his throat. "Hold on to that recipe for sure. And I will update the chief about this development. But I think this angle with the necklace is the clue we need to focus on right now."

Andy had a point. Unlike the recipe, the necklace had a clear link to the murder. But this seemed important too. Maybe just because I was absolutely sick at the thought of Betsy as the killer.

After I hung up with Andy, Elizabeth and I discussed the case some more as we unpacked a large box of donated bedsheets, checking them for stains and tears.

"You said that Ned was feeling tired that day at the

bakery with his workers being out," said Elizabeth. She struggled to refold a fitted sheet. "Maybe that's the reason he was a little weird. It could be he was jealous that Lillian—and not him—was getting a vacation."

"Possible," I said.

As Lillian also had been, Ned was among the sizeable subset of our merchants who rarely took time off. Some in Somerset Harbor liked to claim there was no reason to leave town since we already lived in the most gorgeous place on earth.

Ned had once explained his staying put in another way. "The owner's presence in the kitchen," he had told me, "means a customer receives a perfect cupcake every time." He wanted to be there to check the freshness of ingredients, the consistency of each bowl of batter, the preciseness of the measurements, and other details.

"You know what this means, right?" Elizabeth took out another sheet and gave me a wink. "You and I get an excuse to go to The Fish House. Early dinner Wednesday night?" Our part-timer would be closing, meaning Elizabeth and I could take off early unless the store got slammed.

I smiled. "Do you think they still have that crostini with the bacon jam and brie? No matter, it's a date."

Sleuthing, I had found, had its privileges. And all this talk of cupcakes had me hungry.

Two days later, I was shelving books when Betsy tapped my shoulder and leaned in for a hug.

"Betsy! How's it going?" I asked her with a smile. Despite the chill washing over me, I forced myself to return the embrace.

"Oh, just the usual," she said, then her eyes grew wide. "But oh, that book you sold me! I just devoured that book. I stayed up way too late two nights in a row, so if they catch me snoozing at my desk today, that will be on you," she added with a laugh. "I was really hoping I could steal you away for lunch so we could talk about that ending, which I did not see coming. So much to talk about with this one."

The chill became a tight knot in my stomach at the idea of lunch. Could I just sit there in a restaurant, spearing olives and red onions from a salad bowl while I chatted with a woman who might have done something so inhuman, so unthinkably evil? Had she been questioned by the cops? What was going on? As much as I was dying for an update, I had not reached out that day to Andy, who was working crazy hours.

"Lunch at Asher's? It's on me." Betsy raised a brow, brushing a long strand of hair from her eyes.

"I...well, you know...I'm thinking that I might..." I

swallowed hard, fitting a book into its place on the shelf and taking extra time to make sure it was straight. "It's a little busy here!" Which was true enough. Today was our annual buy-two-paperbacks-and-get-one-free event. The aisles had been crowded and the store abuzz with talk of Lillian's service, held the day before.

"Oh, Rue, please say yes!" Betsy clasped her hands. "Because, Rue—that book, that ending! I have so many thoughts."

The way she rocked on her heels when she was excited reassured me this was Betsy, the same friend I'd always known. The fun-filled Betsy Lawrence, who'd steal an egg roll off my plate and giggle like a twelve-year-old. But who was also known for her thoroughness and brilliance in the courtroom.

Surely there was an explanation for the necklace that would ease my mind.

"Thank you, by the way," I said, "for the nice donation. Looks like you did some winnowing in your jewelry box."

Now, here would come the part where she'd say the jewelry came from others in her office. She'd simply been just the one who'd taken charge of boxing up donations from the group and bringing them into the store when she came in to shop.

"Oh, Rue." She lowered her voice as she grabbed my

arm. "You would not believe it. I had *so much* jewelry that, I swear, is even older than those girls over there." She nodded toward two twenty-something-year-old customers in the science-fiction aisle. "It was way past time to say goodbye to those necklaces and bracelets, time for some new stuff."

So much for reassurance. Her arm on my hand made my skin kind of crawl.

The cops had found no fingerprints on the donated necklace, Andy had reported when he dropped by the store the day before to pick up the recipe as possible evidence in the case. Possibly my own handling of the necklace had smudged any fingerprints that might have told them something. However, William from the Clean and Bright had confirmed to Andy that the necklace matched the one Lillian had been wearing on the morning of the day she died.

I needed to find out when and why my judge friend had gotten her hands on that necklace.

As distasteful as a lunch date felt, some girl talk could be enlightening, maybe helpful for police.

I looked around the store, where we seemed to have hit a lull after a busy morning. I called out to Elizabeth in the Antiquities corner of the store. "Heading out to lunch with Betsy! I'll try to make it quick."

She gave me a raised eyebrow followed by a nod. She knew what I was up to, and I knew she wished me luck.

Betsy grinned and grabbed my hand. She lowered her voice to a whisper. "Let's go talk murder, girl!"

My heart almost stopped until it dawned on me: *The book! She is talking, of course, about the book!*

Arm in arm we headed out the door and down the sidewalk to our lunch.

CHAPTER FIVE

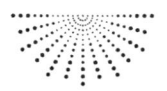

Our favorite waitress, Sharon, set some garlic knots in the middle of the table as the steam and buttery aroma rose to greet us.

"How are you doing, ladies?" Sharon asked. "Sad days here in town!"

Across from me in the vinyl booth, Betsy took a sip of water. "Just sickening," she said. "And just a few blocks from all of us. How could that even happen?"

"I love all my customers." Sharon bit her lip. "But Lillian might have been my favorite, and I was excited for her. I sensed something new was up with her the last time she was in." A small smile crossed the lips of the waitress, and she lowered her voice. "Lillian didn't talk about it," Sharon said, "but I got the idea she had begun to see a male companion in the last few weeks."

Now, that was something new. I leaned forward in my seat. "Do you know who it was?" I asked.

Lillian had maintained that her late husband Hugh was her one great love. "And I won't be so selfish as to ask God for another," she had once said to me. "I am happy these days keeping company with my memories, my cats, and, of course, my books."

But sometimes when I asked about her weekends, I could sense a hole in Lillian's life. On a few occasions I had asked her if she had purchased tickets to a local garden tour or seen one of the stellar shows our local symphony put on. She would just shake her head and tell me that Vivaldi or daylilies were best enjoyed by two.

"I have no clue who it was," said Sharon, "but Lillian seemed quite smitten, a little girlish even. It was kind of fun to see." She smiled at us sadly. "You two should have seen her. She was so shy about it, but also very happy. I would have never guessed about this development! Except I overheard her on the phone thanking some man for some flowers. And I heard her tell him that she was looking forward to a concert they were going to."

The three of us were silent for a minute. Life, it seemed, had tossed out something special to our Lillian, and then some piece of scum had whisked it all away.

"I'll be right back with some menus," Sharon said as she turned to leave.

"Good for Lillian," I told Betsy as I reached for a piece of bread.

"Very nice." She smiled. "Lillian managed to do two things that are, honestly, impossible in this town: keeping a big secret from all the busybodies and finding a good man."

"You got that right," I said. Not that I hadn't had some okay dates here in Massachusetts. I'd found kind men and handsome men. I'd found men who shared my interests and my sense of humor, but in the end, there was no spark.

"How about you?" I asked. "No appealing single lawyers in the courthouse who have caught your eye?" Betsy, I would think, could have her pick, being an attractive woman, top of her class at Boston University School of Law, and able to debate any topic at a cocktail party. Also perhaps a felon, but that remained to be seen.

"Been there and done that," she said. "I fell pretty hard one time when I was young. Got my heart stomped on pretty badly, and at some point, I decided I'd be married to the law." She sipped her drink and frowned. "You don't have to wonder if the law is lying through its teeth. Or if the law will one day ghost you with no warning—poof—and then just disappear."

"In the meantime, if you'd like to *read* about

romance, the best book boyfriend of all time is Jamie Fraser from *Outlander*," I said, leaning in. I had done a blog post on that topic about three weeks before. A huge chunk of our readers were big fans of romances.

After Sharon took our orders, the talk turned to the thriller that had fascinated Betsy. Then once our food appeared, I got down to business as I dug into my salad. First, I wanted to determine if she had an alibi for the window of time in which the crime had taken place.

"So, did you get out at all that day?" I asked her. "Because I just keep thinking I could have passed the monster on the way to the bank or whatever, and that gives me the creeps."

"I do remember that my schedule was really packed that day." She brushed some hair off of her shoulders. "I was stuck there in the courthouse almost the whole day." She seemed to consider something. "But, actually, I managed to get out very briefly...to take care of...something." She picked up her sandwich. "Sometimes you just have to get outside, you know? And just breathe the air."

Normally well-spoken, she was tripping over words to keep from telling me the nature of this "something" that had pulled her from the courthouse. But even if she was hiding something, she was too smart to lie about the fact that she'd gone out that day. As a professional in the field of law, she knew how many witnesses and even cameras might have been watching her as she exited the courthouse and made her way around the town.

I took a deep breath and continued. "Every time I try to sleep, I just keep seeing Lillian's face." I took a sip of coffee. "Did you know Lillian well?"

"I really wish I had, but I met her only once. We both had volunteered to do some landscaping downtown. A few years ago, I think." Betsy picked up a triangle of club sandwich. "I found her to be delightful."

Met her only once, she'd said. But Elizabeth had photos that told another story. Most of the items in Elizabeth's corner of the shop were from decades past, but she had some more recent photos too, mostly from the nearby area. Sometimes following a death, she would pull some photos and news clippings for the family and mail them out, compliments of Antiquities by Elizabeth. Currently, she was in the process of culling any items she could find that had a connection to the beloved seamstress.

I'd looked at them just that morning, and there in living color were Lillian and Betsy smiling at each other, working as a team to take admissions tickets at a fashion show. In another photo, Betsy was shown whispering in Lillian's ear at a festival downtown. Apparently, they'd also worked together in a play, according to an old

A DONATION OF MURDER

theater program in Elizabeth's collection. Both their names were listed as part of a hair-and-makeup crew at the Glove and Garter, the local playhouse here in town.

Elizabeth and I had stared hard at the items, wondering when the animosity had started—if there *had been* animosity between the two of them, enough to drive a respected judge to murder.

Why wouldn't she just say that she had worked with Lillian on projects around town?

As we finished up the meal, I pressed a little harder about this relationship with Lillian that Betsy was pretending she had never had.

I leaned back in my seat. "I can't believe I won't be seeing Lillian when I drop off my clothes. What a tremendous loss." I paused. "Do you use the Clean and Bright?"

"If I need dry cleaning, then that is where I go. So close! But it's honestly not often that I have the need," she said with a shrug. "Life is just easier, you know, when you look for clothes that you can wash at home."

I reached for my glass of water, and I swallowed hard because a memory rushed at me. Before I had been startled by the necklace in her box of donations, I'd eyed with much excitement a neatly folded stack of skirts and blouses underneath the jewelry pouch. The ones on top were wrapped in sheaths of plastic with "Capable Cleaners" scrolled across the top in black cursive letters. That dry-cleaning business was on the other side of town from where Betsy lived and worked. It was like she had been *avoiding* the place where Lillian worked.

Betsy had just told me her second lie that day.

CHAPTER SIX

When I got back to the store, Elizabeth had a line at the register. Our young staffer Dorie had arrived and was busy at another, so I rushed to the front to open a new station.

An ecstatic Gatsby was standing in a knot of admiring women. I gave one of them a wink as I passed. "He's such a ladies' man," I teased. "I think more people come here to see Gatsby than they do to buy books."

The staff worked steadily to take payments and bag books while Oliver dozed, oblivious, at the end of the counter. Into each bag I stuck a bookmark advertising our visiting authors for the next few months.

After we'd checked out the last customers in line, Dorie moved away to speak to a teenage boy who seemed to need some help in the biographies.

I turned to Elizabeth. "There will be a lot of reading going on tonight. It's been quite a day for sales."

"And for other things as well," she said in a whisper. "I can't wait to hear about your lunch."

"It was interesting," I said. I'd have to fill her in once the store was closed and we were alone.

"Oh, and by the way, go check out my table in Antiquities when you get a chance," she said. Since we'd found the Fish House recipe, she'd been looking through her files for any photographs or information she could find on Ned's grandmother Kate.

Anxious to take a peek, I headed off in that direction, stopping along the way to greet customers in the aisles and make book suggestions. When I made it back to Antiquities by Elizabeth, I could see right away what she'd set out for me to see. It was a yellowed page from a newspaper with obituaries sandwiched between ads for Reeboks, insurance, and pork chops.

In the middle of the page was the one I wanted: Kate Julianna Lansing, age sixty-one, died July 28, 1981, here in Somerset Harbor.

How on earth had Elizabeth pulled off that discovery? Such a random thing to find! I'd been online to no avail for the obituary.

Very carefully, I picked up the fragile paper. For such a vibrant and accomplished woman, the obit was short and simple. Kate, I learned, had been born in Black Wolf, Wisconsin. With no mention of a husband or a marriage, the only survivors listed were Ned and his father. Kate, according to the obit, had enjoyed long walks, card games, and crossword puzzles. A few odd jobs were listed, including a short stint as a coat-check girl at The Waltzing Chickadee, a once popular nightclub here in town.

Oddly, there was no mention of her heroic nursing work in World War Two or her love for baking. She wasn't yet a legend in the New England foodie world. That distinction would only come following her death when her grandson made her signature dessert into a much-heralded sensation.

But still, she had lived a large life, and in these scant paragraphs, Kate Lansing seemed so small.

Then a voice behind me pulled me out of my thoughts. "Who did your highlights, girl? You must have a genius stylist."

I turned around to see a grinning Tiffany, her arms filled with paperbacks.

"My stylist is okay," I told her with a wink. "I imagine that I'll keep her."

Today Tiffany was wearing a pink jean jacket over a short black dress with flirty ruffles at the bottom.

I pulled her aside. "Do you know what I heard today?

Today I heard that Lillian might have been seeing someone." I kept my voice very low. "Do you think that's true?"

She smiled. "I thought it was a secret. But actually, she was. She kind of let it slip not too long ago, but she wouldn't tell me who. She wanted to, you know, just keep it to herself. To see where it might go."

"That makes sense," I said. There were people here who made a pastime out of knowing everybody's business, and you had to make an effort not to say too much. I could see the wisdom of keeping to yourself a new relationship that may or may not stick.

"It sounded so romantic." Tiffany leaned against a shelf. "And I got the idea he was an awesome guy. He took her to a cooking class last month in Provincetown! They made homemade pizza."

"Pizza!" squawked the parrot.

Several browsers startled, and others looked around with knowing smiles.

A small boy in the children's section tugged on his mother's skirt. "Can we get pizza, Mom? Can we get extra cheese?"

I shot an apologetic glance in her direction, and she laughed and shook her head.

"We'll see," she told the boy.

Then I turned to Tiffany. "I'm sure you did your best

A DONATION OF MURDER

to get the name of this supposed new man in her life."

"Oh, yeah, you know I tried," she said with a laugh. Then she gazed around at the busy aisles. "Have any of your customers today heard anything at all that they've passed along?" she asked. "About the investigation?"

"Unfortunately, no." I crossed my arms over my chest, staring at the new sign taped up to the front desk. It was asking people to come forward if they'd seen or talked to Lillian on the day of her murder or the day before.

"I can't believe," I said, "that some of her customers with appointments on that day still haven't spoken up."

Maybe they liked paperbacks; maybe they'd come into the Seabreeze, see the sign, and finally get the message. The signs had been distributed the day after the murder by the merchants guild.

Tiffany rolled her eyes. "Yeah, it really stinks they won't step up and help. Even if they think they don't know something that could help, you never really know. Lillian's family deserves that little bit of time it would take somebody to answer a few questions."

"Well, let me get back to the register," I said, noticing a line had begun to form again. "I'm thinking we should do this sale with paperbacks maybe twice a year. Or maybe even three." This was turning out to be a huge day for sales.

We worked steadily at the register, complimenting customers on their choice of books and suggesting other titles whose themes were similar. When the last customer in line had walked away happily with three books in the *Divergent* series, Elizabeth and I made our way to the tea cart for a needed break.

"Good job on the obit," I told her quietly. "I'm in awe of your skills."

"It was fairly simple, really." She took a sip of tea. "I was thinking back on a conversation that I once had with Ned—about royal weddings, of all things. This was way back when Prince Harry married Meghan."

"What in the world?" I asked. How was that a clue?

"He told me his grandmother was a major fan of the royal family, royal weddings, all of that," Elizabeth continued. "Kate, it turned out, was obsessed way back in the day with all the wedding prep for Charles and Diana. And Ned was telling me how mad she would have been if she had only known that she would die that very week."

I took a sip. "Oh no."

"By only a few days, she would miss her chance to see her beloved Diana become a royal princess," said Elizabeth. "So, because of that, I had a good idea about when she would have died—and I file my stuff by year."

"Some of that stuff was interesting," I said.

"As was the stuff that got left out."

"Fish House tonight?" I asked.

She nodded as she smiled at a customer who was balancing an armful of books. "Let me get you a basket," said Elizabeth as she hurried toward the front.

I made my way to the register, where Dorie was busy once again.

Next in line was Tiffany, who had filled a basket to almost overflowing with her paperback selections.

"These should keep you busy for a year," I told her with a laugh as I began to unpack her books onto the counter.

My friend shrugged. "Well, you always say never to get caught without a book in your purse."

"In case of an emergency." I nodded. It was a bit of wisdom I passed on to all my customers. Stuck in the doctor's waiting room or waiting for a friend who was late for lunch? A book was a companion at the ready in your purse, a friend on the page who was probably in the middle of some drama you were eager to dive into.

"I see I taught you well." I smiled at Tiffany as I began to scan her books.

Admiring her oversized hoop earrings, I made a mental note to check out when I could go through that box of donations Tiffany had packed. Her stuff was always stylish, and I wondered if she might have put some cute shoes in there. I was really in the mood for a new pair of boots, and the price of boots in the store across the street had almost made me lose my breath when I checked the week before. This was a fun town to browse in, but the merchandise was known for its quality and uniqueness, not for the bargain prices.

That is why when we had another lull in business, I went to find that box, which I remembered had the name of one of her suppliers, Curl Sophisticate. And I was in luck. While there were no books, there was a cute pair of red heels, low enough that I could wear them in the store, where I was very often on my feet all day. And they were my size!

What else had she packed? Digging past some skirts, I pulled out a portfolio. Some lucky customer at the Foundation sale would snatch it up for sure. It seemed to be real leather, judging from the feel and smell, and there were no scratches. Opening it up, I checked all the pockets for anything she might have left inside, which happened all the time.

It was surprising, really, what people had accidentally "donated" to the cause. Some of them, for instance, had failed to check the pockets of the coats or pants they'd thrown inside a box. Items had gotten left in the compartments of purses and tote bags. So far, we'd found two ten-dollar bills, a scratch-off lottery ticket with a fifteen-dollar prize, and (whoops) someone's driver's license.

Tiffany's stuff, I figured, was especially worth a careful check. Her overeager mind was sometimes a big jumble of things she must do now and things she had to tell you. Important details in the process sometimes got overlooked.

Sure enough, in a back pocket of the portfolio were three fashion sketches. I studied the pictures one by one. They were intricately detailed, signed neatly at the bottom...and very, very bad. Taken aback, I stared at the penciled ladies wearing outfits I would never, ever wear. Surely no one would. Suddenly, I understood why Tiffany had failed to move ahead in her chosen field.

It made me a little sick to know her dream was likely futile. In her eyes I saw the hunger and the spark I'd had at her age. I recognized in her the longing to do the work she loved. I'd found where I belonged here at the Seabreeze, and I wanted that for her. But she would not be finding it, not in the fashion world.

Next, with a heavy heart, I pulled out some scarves and tops, followed by a gray Tory Burch tote bag.

I studied the bag and, wow, she was letting herself part with some awesome stuff. Which was great for the Foundation.

And also for me.

A lot of books would fit in that.

I carefully unzipped it so I could check the lining—and my careless friend had done it once again. Several bits of paper had been left inside. Most of them were unimportant: a torn stub from a movie, a receipt from Sushi Time. But the next item that I pulled out made me gasp. It was an appointment card to be measured for a fitting at the Clean and Bright—at 3:30 p.m. on March 3, the day of Lillian's death. "Skirt hemmed," said the card, and that made Tiffany the last person who was known to have seen Lillian alive. Tiffany—who had just joined in my complaints about the "mystery customers" who had failed to step up and help with the investigation.

I closed my eyes and breathed, fitting this piece of news into the confusing set of facts that had come to light so far.

My seamstress friend was dead.

My stylist was hiding something in connection to the brutal scissor slashing that had rocked our town.

And my thriller reading buddy might have pulled a move from one of our darker reads.

Normally, this might be just the time to lose myself in a sugary concoction that would melt right in my mouth. But my favorite baker was keeping secrets too.

I sent a text to Andy: "For 'Skirt Hemmed at 3:30,' I can fill in the blank."

CHAPTER SEVEN

The interior of The Fish House was all old-school glamour: white tablecloths and candles and comfy upholstered booths. The crowd was pretty decent for a Wednesday night, but it wasn't like the old days when my gran and grandpa would take me out to eat as a child during my summer visits to the beach. Back then we'd sometimes wait an hour for a table, but, oh, what a treat. I had especially loved the orange sherbet for dessert, served in a fancy glass bowl with a chocolate fish on top.

While Elizabeth and I perused the menu, the wine steward joined us to introduce the wine list. There was a lovely Chenin blanc, he said, as well as an oaky Chardonnay of which he was especially fond. "We also have some interesting mixed drinks that you'll see on the menu," he added with a smile. "May I help with some suggestions?"

While his face was relatively unlined and his step fairly quick, a closer look made me believe this man might be in his eighties. What I really wanted out of tonight's excursion was a little chat with someone who had been around The Fish House for a while. Now here was a man who had lived a long life, and if I was lucky, many of those years would have been spent working within these walls.

When I told him I was considering the lobster ravioli, he suggested that I try the restaurant's newest red blend from California.

That sounded good to us, and we said we'd take a bottle.

While we were waiting, I gave Elizabeth a quiet update on my lunch with Betsy.

"Why the lies?" she asked, her eyes growing wide as I finished with my summary.

"It blows my mind," I said. "Something's up with her for sure. And with Tiffany! I need to fill you in on her. It's like I'm seeing a new side of everyone I know."

"Tiffany too?" she asked.

I described the surprises that I found in her donation box, finishing the story as our waitress arrived to take our orders. She was followed quickly by the elderly wine steward, who uncorked our bottle.

I carefully took a sip and nodded my approval. "Very good," I told him.

"I am so glad to hear it, and my name is Carl. Please just ask for me if I can be of further service."

"Have you worked here long?" asked Elizabeth, reaching for her glass.

"This is my 'retirement job,'" he told us with a chuckle. "I was in the finance field in Boston, but wine has always been my passion, and I have fond memories of this place from my days as a boy. My father, in fact, was the manager for the longest time, and I would hang out here if they couldn't find a sitter. Dad would set me up at a table in the back, and I'd sit there for hours and color. I'd do lots of puzzles. The staff was very kind, and, of course, there were the treats."

Yes! I needed details on the treats, one in particular.

"Would you believe that I'm already dreaming of dessert even though I just ordered my entrée?" I asked him with a laugh. "I don't suppose a fancy place like this would have a cupcake on the menu? I kind of have a craving."

"I don't believe they do." He paused for a moment as a memory seemed to make his blue eyes go soft. "But back in the day, our chef Melissa made a cupcake you would not believe. She liked to experiment, you see. One day you'd taste a slice of caramel layer cake, and it would be superb but not quite to her standards. The next day you might taste a different version that was slightly better but still missing something, according to Melissa. She would keep on trying until she got a recipe just the way she wanted." He grinned from ear to ear. "She allowed me to believe I was her chief taste tester, quite the honor for a lad!"

"And there was a cupcake?" asked Elizabeth.

Carl closed his eyes, and his voice grew soft. "One in particular that I still dream about after all these years. It is still, I believe, the most exquisite bite of food I have ever tasted—and I have had the fortune of dining in some world-class eateries."

"Well, it really is a shame it's not on the menu now," I said.

"Tragically, the recipe for that version became lost. Melissa was a genius in the kitchen but also somewhat scattered." He let out a sigh. "She tried really hard but could never replicate those beyond-perfect cupcakes that she served one magical afternoon back in the 1940s."

"A perfect *key-lime* cupcake?" asked Elizabeth.

His eyebrows shot up in surprise. "How could you possibly know that?" he asked.

A DONATION OF MURDER

"We're from Somerset Harbor," I explained. "Home of the *famous* key-lime cupcakes—from The Cupcakery. So when we think of special cupcakes, that's where our minds go."

"Yes, I've heard of those, but I've never tried one," he told us. "Once you've tasted perfect, it's awfully hard to be satisfied with a lesser version. No offense, of course!" he was quick to add. "I've been to The Cupcakery with family, but I always order the Chocolate-Vanilla Swirl, which I do enjoy."

Once he had stepped away, Elizabeth grabbed my hand. "I was really hoping that it wasn't true!" she said. "That the recipe was Kate's, just like we've always heard."

It was a heartwarming story, part of our town lore, and this felt like a loss.

Elizabeth frowned. "That story we just heard really makes it look like Ned's been lying all along."

"But how would Ned have even gotten that old recipe from the nineteen forties?" I asked her quietly. "He would not have even been alive back when it was lost."

"Maybe Kate's the one who found it. Then Ned opened up the business and made a story up about the recipe, one that customers would like," she said.

Which would make Ned a fraud; he had the written

recipe with the Fish House name across the top.

Had Lillian figured it all out and confronted him about it? Maybe she had done it the day before she died, when she had grabbed those cupcakes for the staff at Reba's House of Beauty?

But how on earth would Lillian figure out a thing like that?

Elizabeth took a sip of wine, and she seemed to read my mind. "Are you trying in your mind to connect this to the murder?" she asked softly. Like everyone who worked downtown, we couldn't seem to get the death off our minds.

I nodded.

"If we could figure out," said Elizabeth, "who the boyfriend is, maybe he's the link. He came into her life, it seems, not long before she died."

"That makes sense," I said. "And it's possible, of course, that this stuff with the cupcakes is unconnected to the murder."

Which would mean our poor town was about to be dealing with two scandals at one time.

As soon as I got home, I called Andy's cell. "Get over here right now," I said. "There's clam chowder from The Fish House that I brought for you." I knew him well enough to know he was likely skipping meals, and he'd been looking even more worn-out than he usually got working a big case. He would have to watch that, given the tendency for his blood-pressure numbers to shoot up through the roof when he tried to do too much.

Fifteen minutes later, he appeared, much to the delight of Gatsby, who spun in happy circles until he was calm enough to take the treat from Andy's outstretched hand.

"Rue, you're very kind," said Andy. "I didn't realize I was starving until you said those magic words—clam chowder."

We sat on the porch and talked while he dug into his meal. "So, you have information," he began, "about one of the unknown persons who was at the Clean and Bright?"

When I told him what I'd found, he was as shocked and confused as I had been.

"We'll talk to Tiffany for sure," he said, adding that the chief had called in Betsy earlier that evening for an interview. No mention had been made to her about the necklace. The idea, Andy said, was to ask their questions first before showing her their hand. Once she knew they had the necklace, she might very well clam up.

The chief had told her they were being thorough, talking to as many people as they could who were downtown at the time. He also said they'd had a tip that they should question her, that she might know something.

"That is when she started to get nervous," Andy said.

"Yes, I can imagine."

"But she did give him an idea about her whereabouts that day." Andy took another bite. "The judge maintained to the chief that she'd had a full day at the courthouse on the day that Lillian died. She later sent her schedule, and, just as she had told him, it was pretty packed."

I met Andy's eyes. "Did she specifically tell the chief that she never left the building during the hours when the murder could have taken place?"

He paused with his spoon halfway to his mouth. "That was implied," he said.

I let out a sigh, because the chief of all people should have known to be specific with his questions, especially with a savvy suspect.

I myself had been careful with my phrasing when I put the question to her: *Did you get out at all that day?* And it had brought a yes, as opposed to a *non-answer* about how busy she had been.

"She *did* leave the building on the day that Lillian died!" I announced to Andy.

Andy swallowed hard and raised a brow.

"She told me that today. The two of us had lunch."

"Oh, yes, I know you did. You had lunch at Asher's. We've been keeping a close watch on the judge's activities since that necklace surfaced." His eyes looked alert. "Where did she tell you that she went on the day of the murder?"

I explained the vagueness of her answer. "I could kind of tell she didn't want to say, but she left the building, that's for sure."

"Very interesting," he said.

"Lots of people acting weird." I leaned back in my chair. "But are you any closer to arresting someone? Please tell me that you are."

He took a bite of bread. "I wish I could say yes. We're doing all we can: monitoring the tip line, checking any security footage we can find from the downtown shops, looking into Lillian's past for anything at all that might stick out as a motive."

"I hear she had a man." I bent to scoop up Beasley and hold him in my lap.

"That is true. She did," said Andy with a nod. "But she kept that kind of private, so I will honor Lillian's wishes when it comes to that." He gave me a small smile. "You do have a way, Rue, of getting information." He picked up his napkin and dabbed at his mouth.

"Have you interviewed this man?" I asked.

"He's every bit as anxious as everybody else to see this thing get solved. And, yes, he has disclosed anything he knows that might be useful." Andy started on the piece of cheesecake that I'd brought him. Then he pushed the takeout box across the table to offer me a bite.

Having been smart enough to ask at The Fish House for a second fork, I dug into the cheesecake and gave Andy a sad smile. "It sounds like she was on a kick to start living her best life: a trip to France, a new look, and a man."

He gave me a wry smile. "And even with all of that, we've come to understand she still had time to go chasing UFOs."

"*What?*" I almost spit out my cheesecake.

"I could not believe it either," Andy said, "but that's our latest message from the anonymous tip line." He shoved another bite of dessert into his mouth. "Lillian supposedly got into a heated argument with another woman in Mulberry Park not long before she died. And this argument took place following a gathering of a special-interest group that goes by the name UFO Believers."

"But that is not at all a Lillian kind of thing," I said. Surely that was wrong! In her time as a customer, she had special-ordered a lot of fact-based books by respected thinkers in the field of science—books on ecology, for example.

"Maybe she was just walking in the park that day," I said, "and happened to run into one of these...believers."

"Those were my thoughts too at first." Andy leaned back in his chair. "But it was supposedly a rainy night at around ten o'clock. There was nothing open at that time in that part of town except for that little building in the park where groups sometimes meet." He shrugged. "It's possible, of course, the tipster was a fake. People have been known to make up stories to insert themselves into a case that's been in the news. But I listened to the tape, and my gut is telling me the tip's legitimate."

"But why?"

"There was a mention, for one thing, of a purple-striped umbrella that Lillian had that day. Not a lot of people knew that Lillian sometimes carried one of those."

"What was the argument about?"

"The caller didn't say."

"If she's legitimate," I said, "why would she not show up in person, answer questions, all of that? Have you tried to interview these flying-saucer people?" It kind of blew my mind that really was a thing.

"We are trying at the moment to scout some of them

out," said Andy. "They're rather secretive from what I understand."

I touched my nose to Beasley's, then snuggled the cat closer to my chest. "Ah, a *secret* group. That sounds like a challenge."

He gave me a look I was very used to. "You be careful, Rue. One of them, for all we know, could have been the person who came after Lillian with those scissors like a maniac. You leave that to the cops."

I, of course, had no intention of going after them, but that didn't mean I couldn't do a little sleuthing to unmask them.

"You're sounding like yourself again," I told Andy even as ideas floated in my head about how to find the people in our town who believed in flying saucers.

How many of them could there be?

CHAPTER EIGHT

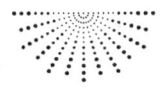

*T*he next day I was setting up a display of mugs with literary quotes when Charla from the parks department called me back. I understood from Andy the department kept no records about who used the room where the Believers sometimes met at Mulberry Park. But I was hoping someone who worked at the park might have seen the group as they came and went. All I needed was one name.

If I could figure out a way to pop into a Believers gathering, maybe I could pinpoint someone in the group who might have had a motive to go after Lillian. But the times and meeting places varied every month to maintain secrecy—which I didn't get. Sure, some might not agree with what the Believers thought, but it wasn't like these people were doing something wrong.

"Hey, girl, I got your message," Charla told me cheerfully. "We've been missing you and Gatsby lately on our walks."

Charla and I had become good friends on the nature walks she led at the smallish park behind my house, one of several parks scattered around town. On most nights after the walks, I'd stay and let Gatsby run around with Charla's Dalmatian, Fred. While we watched "the kids" play, we'd have some fun debates, ranging from which Adele song was the best to which boyfriend Rory should have ended up with on *The Gilmore Girls*.

"I do miss you guys, and I need the exercise," I said. "Being busy at the store is absolutely no excuse, so we'll be back for sure." Then I took a breath. "Okay, Charla, listen. There's a group I understand has met a time or two in that little building in Mulberry Park. I think they go by the name The UFO Believers. Would you happen by any chance to know a contact person? Or someone who's involved?"

That was followed by a pause. "Oh!" Charla said, surprised. Then she cleared her throat. "Rue, I understand that people might have seen things that cannot be explained. But don't you think there are explanations that make a lot more sense than other beings swooping down to check out life on Earth? You have to see that, right?"

"Oh, I don't want to join! That's not the reason that I called!" How humiliating.

"The better explanations for unexplained phenomena are fluctuations in the temperature or some type of debris," she said. Charla regularly scooped up stacks of books from our nonfiction aisles, and she seemed to remember every fact she ever read. "Although airborne clutter is a whole lot less exciting than a visitor from Venus," she continued, "that is simply science, Rue."

"You don't need to convince me, because I get it, Charla."

The fiery assistant to the rec director loved a good debate. A good debate, in fact, was the foundation of our friendship, but on this topic, we agreed. I was having enough trouble with the earthly beings in my life; I didn't need *more* people from distant galaxies to complicate things even more.

"No way do I think aliens are real," I assured my friend. "Although, if some of them took a notion to beam themselves into Massachusetts in the off-season months, I wouldn't push away their Mastercards."

"Aren't you funny, Rue? And I'm sorry, no. I don't have a contact. I had no idea this group even existed."

Well, shoot. I searched my mind for a plan B. Perhaps the hobby store over on the east side. It sold telescopes!

Was that the way it worked? Did Believers congregate to stand out in some open field to look for flying saucers or maybe flashing lights?

I had no idea.

"Got to go!" said Charla, "but get yourself to the park, or else I'm gonna have to bring Fred into the store to get his Gatsby fix."

"You know Gatsby would love it. I will catch you soon," I told her, hanging up.

Frowning, I centered a yellow mug into the display. How to find these secret searchers of beings from afar?

"I'll think about that tomorrow," proclaimed the yellow mug, which featured Scarlett O'Hara looking all serene under her wide beribboned hat. Yes! Scarlett was the character I felt like channeling that day. Tomorrow, after all, was another chance to hit upon the perfect plan.

With the mug display all finished, I headed to the back for a box of handmade bookmarks that had recently arrived. As I entered the back room, I had to squeeze through the growing stacks of donation boxes to reach the merchandise. Thank goodness the sale was getting close, but I was glad those boxes had been there to offer up their hints about the donors' lives. Despite the carefully selected bestsellers in the front, it had been the discards that had told the most important stories of the week.

They'd told other tales as well, intriguing little peeks at other lives. There had been, for instance, some well-read racy paperbacks contributed by the uptight, always slightly angry front desk clerk at my optometrist's. The burly UPS man had apparently collected—and then given up—a variety of items with a chicken theme. There were plastic cups and watches with brightly colored chickens. There were chickens who clucked when you pulled their strings, and chickens who laid plastic eggs.

As I grabbed the bookmarks, I began to wonder if Lillian might have dropped some donations off as well. There had been very few community endeavors that she had not enthusiastically supported. I paused to scan the boxes and overstuffed plastic bags, wondering how I'd ever pick hers out from the jumble.

"Lillian, speak to me," I said under my breath, and that is when I saw it toward the bottom of a stack: a box labeled "Bellingham, the Connoisseur's Choice for Chocolate."

I gasped. Could it be? The pricey chocolates in the signature blue foil had been Lillian's one indulgence, tiny rich and creamy bites to sweeten up her otherwise super healthy diet of lean proteins, fruit, and salads.

Once a year or so, she'd have a giant box shipped in from New York. Sometimes, after she'd been in for some books, I'd look down and discover a chocolate on the counter. Filled with berry-flavored creme or perhaps salted caramel, these candies were exquisite, and the surprise of finding one always made my day.

That box *had* to have come from Lillian. Bellingham was a boutique chocolatier that was little known in Massachusetts. Lillian had told me once that it was a secret that New Yorkers liked to keep to themselves.

I unstacked the bags and boxes until I could get to it, then I peeked into the store to make sure I wasn't needed. Just two customers were browsing, and in case they had any questions, Elizabeth was close by, sorting through some postcards for her section of the shop.

After opening the box, the first thing I pulled out was a blue cashmere scarf I'd seen Lillian wear on chilly winter days. Was it my imagination, or did it have a hint of the sandalwood perfume Lillian sometimes wore? I decided right away I would keep that scarf.

Digging further into the neatly packed donations, I found a couple of coffee table books with a fashion theme along with several blouses, a couple of coffee mugs, a pitcher, and a box of note cards that featured hand-painted ocean scenes.

"Nice," I whispered to myself as I lifted the plastic lid

from the box of cards. Then I peeked inside the top card to see that my late friend was among the contributors who'd failed to double-check their gifts. She'd apparently scratched out the beginning of a note and then began again, scratching out and rewriting as she went.

"Sorry is a small word for the grave misjudgment that I made," Lillian had written. "Please know that I think every day about what might have been and what was lost because of me. Wishing you bells and apple blossoms. In regret and friendship, Lillian."

Bells? And apple blossoms?

There was no name for the addressee, but there was a date, and the note was written eight days before she died.

I carefully set it down and got Andy on the phone.

He picked up right away and sounded more upbeat than normal. His tone was even teasing. "Don't tell me. Let me guess," he said with a chuckle. "You're sorting through another box, and now you've solved the case."

"Well, I haven't *solved* it, but I've found a motive maybe."

He didn't answer right away.

"I was only kidding!" Andy said when he could finally speak. "Rue, what do you have?"

"I have a note. From Lillian! And yes, it's another

clue I found in a box of donations. Let me read it to you."

When I was finished reading, he let out a low whistle.

"This was written, Andy, eight days before she died," I said.

I hated that such a dark picture had begun to form about Lillian's final days. Sure, we all had regrets, but Lillian, I was sure, was being way too hard on herself. I had never known her to be less than kind.

"Just figure out who did it," I told Andy as I gently pulled some gloves out of her box of donations.

"We're really trying, Rue. I'll send someone for that note."

I hung up with Andy and wandered back into the store to find Elizabeth straightening items at her desk. After the big sale on paperbacks, the store that day was quiet.

"Elizabeth," I said, "how would one go about, do you think, finding people in this town who believe in UFOs?"

She looked at me, startled. "Well, now that I wouldn't know." After a pause, she shrugged. "I don't know much about it, but I would not discount life on other planets. It would be a little odd for the only life in the *whole universe* to be right here on Earth, this minuscule percentage of everything there is." There was another thoughtful pause. "But while I do believe in life beyond our planet, that doesn't mean I think those beings, in whatever form they take, are up there zooming in the sky in some flying-saucer thingies."

I held up a hand. "I never said that I believed that! I just want to find the people in this town who do." I looked her in the eye. "There might be a connection—to the murder." Then I explained to Elizabeth what I'd heard from Andy.

"Interesting," she said, thinking for a moment. "Maybe we could look through the list of special orders over the last year, see if something on that topic's been requested."

"Oh, and there's something else," I said. I was telling her about Lillian's note when my phone vibrated in my pocket. When I pulled it out, Tiffany's name flashed across the screen.

"How's it going?" I asked her, walking toward my office.

"Bad day at the salon," she said. "I will need a drink tonight—or two. Meet me at the Pink Whale at eight?"

"That sounds like a plan," I said. Drinks with Tiffany could be kind of perfect for us both. She needed a drink, and I needed to figure out why she was lying through her teeth about when she'd last seen Lillian.

At the thought of Lillian, the loss hit me once again. "It will feel good to get out," I said to Tiffany. "I couldn't sleep last night. I just kept seeing Lillian's face."

"Yeah, it was just horrific what some creep did to her. She could be judgmental. She could be obtuse about the needs of others. But, yeah, it kills me, Rue, to think of her in such pain."

Judgmental? And obtuse when it came to others? As in the "grave misjudgment" described in the note?

Yes, Tiffany and I were due for a chat.

"See you tonight," I said.

CHAPTER NINE

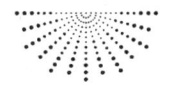

Somehow we managed to grab a table by the window at the bustling Pink Whale. I tried to calm my racing thoughts as I gazed out at the square in the middle of downtown. The daylilies were in full bloom, and the streams of water shooting from the fountain seemed to be made of crystals as the street lights shone on them.

Tiffany took a sip of her second pineapple-mango daiquiri. Then she closed her eyes. "Today was just too much," she said. "First there was a no-show. And then after that, a customer walks in with her hair down to her waist and a million tangles. It took me fifteen minutes just to get them out." She took another sip and leaned back in her chair. "I was thinking to myself, has this full-grown woman never even heard of this thing called a *brush?* Not a new invention."

"Unbelievable." I picked up my drink. "But most days I imagine your job is pretty cool. You get to spend your days making people gorgeous—which you're great at, by the way." In addition to doing hair, she had also started offering her services as a makeup artist.

She took another sip. "Some days I kind of hate it and, Rue, here's the thing. I really do want to help women be transformed into their most amazing selves! But I don't want to do that by adding textured layers to their hair or turning them from brunettes into blondes. The job at the salon? It is so not me. I was born to create with pastel pink chiffon that flows just past a woman's knees. To design show-stopping gowns in silky baby blue." Tiffany's eyes grew dreamy. "A navy cocktail dress that's tea-length, off the shoulder! Very, very classy!" She reached out to touch my hand. "If you are in doubt, you can always go with navy."

A dark look filled her eyes as she downed the rest of her drink. "Not that I will ever get to really *use* this knowledge. Sometimes I'm afraid that when I'm sixty-five, I'll still be stuck at Reba's, struggling to cut the hair of some preteen girl who cannot sit still when a Taylor Swift song plays. Do they not understand I have *scissors* in my hand?"

Both of us caught our breath at the mention of that word.

"Sorry!" Tiffany clapped her hand over her mouth. "That kind of just came out." She scowled and looked down into her empty glass. "What I meant to say is that my life is the worst."

This was a different version of the Tiffany I knew. It wasn't new for her to have a day made up of small disasters. But almost every time by the middle of her first drink, she would have turned her bad day into the kind of story that had us in hysterics.

Not tonight.

Her laser focus on a career in fashion broke my heart. No one with decent vision (or a serviceable pair of glasses) would invest in one of those creations from her portfolio. I pictured the jean jacket that was meant to look "distressed" but instead gave the appearance of being covered up in mold.

I didn't understand! She always looked so cute and put together in the clothes she chose to wear. But, apparently, dressing well and designing well were two separate skills. Someone in her college program should have (very gently) given her some tough advice: dream big, but point your dreams in a new direction.

Since that didn't happen, a friend should probably tell her.

Should that friend be me?

Ouch.

Having no clue what to do, I did what I always did when faced with a dilemma: I ordered myself a plate of something wrapped in bacon.

"You know, I'm kind of craving this shrimp appetizer." I glanced at the menu. "It comes with chimichurri sauce, which would be amazing, and I am a little hungry."

"That sounds good to me," she said. "I'll order the mushroom croquettes and we can share."

We flagged down our waitress to put in the order, then I got down to business. I needed to dig further into Tiffany's relationship with Lillian in the days before her death.

"I still can't believe that Lillian's not around," I said. "I wish I'd seen her more in the weeks before she died. Did you say that day at the salon was the last time that you saw her?"

She twisted some hair around her index finger, her mouth forming a firm line. "Yeah, that was the last time. And, yeah, I get what you're saying. It's hard to get my head around the idea that she's gone."

"And I just keep hoping soon they'll make an arrest," I said. Then I leaned in close. "What do you think is up with those people here in town who were at the Clean

A DONATION OF MURDER

and Bright that day for alterations? And who just *ignores* *police* when they are pleading for those people to please give them a call?"

"Um...I guess I don't really know." Tiffany continued to twirl the long string of hair, this time twisting it so tightly it must surely hurt her scalp.

"Maybe they forgot?" I said with a shrug. "If they were super busy and that was only *one* of a ton of errands they had to run that day." Desperately, I wanted that to be the answer. Perhaps that would jog her memory.

She turned her gaze to me, her eyes growing wide. "No one would forget about a thing like that," she said. "That would be a big deal, picking up some new clothes tailored just for them—to hug their curves just right or be the perfect length. We're talking fashion, Rue, and fashion is important." Then she seemed to snap out of the fashion fervor. "But then, yeah, I guess people do get busy. So maybe they forgot."

Some people might forget if they were not obsessed with clothes. But never Tiffany. No doubt she was lying about the last time she'd seen Lillian. I'd been veering in my mind from seeing her as a likely suspect to thinking she would never in a million years hurt Lillian. But her harsh words about her friend coupled with her blatant lie caused a wave of sickness to rise up in my stomach.

We made a little small talk, both of us subdued, before the waitress came to set our food down on the table. I nodded my thanks, and we declined more drinks. I picked up my fork but then set it down. So crazy how I could lose my appetite completely amid the warm aromas of crisp bacon and the garlic and chili peppers mingling in the sauce.

Lillian had been a patient mentor, answering every question Tiffany had ever thrown at her about a career in fashion. Lillian and I used to shake our heads over how driven and obsessed Tiffany could be over the career she imagined for herself.

"It's not all glitz and glamor," Lillian once told me. "It's demanding clients all day long, insane hours and hard work, a life I was glad to leave." We marveled over the way Tiffany could turn any conversation to the subject of design. If Lillian made a comment about some red and yellow flowers they passed in a park, Tiffany might ask how she'd feel about that color combination in an upscale raincoat. Could Lillian describe the way the hot new colors of each season were determined? And on and on and on.

From Tiffany's recent comments I could tell the relationship to some extent had soured, but what on earth had gone wrong? Time to encourage her to do a little venting.

"I know this is hard for you since you and Lillian were so close," I tried. "What a lucky thing that you and Lillian shared an interest. Kind of like me and my gran. With my love for books, Gran understood before I did that the Seabreeze was the perfect place for me. I wasn't sure that I could do it—be in charge at the store—but she knew all along."

"That's all I need—a chance!" Tiffany's eyes were pleading. "Just like Lillian had. Lillian had her chance to work with the top people who were defining trends! Who were creating pieces that were art as much as fashion. Lillian was right there in the rooms with the magic happening around her!" Her tone turned from fervent to subdued. "I think it was hard for someone with her luck to understand what it's like for me."

I reached for a shrimp and cut a small bite with my fork. "Well, as I understand it, it was more than luck. She put in a lot of time before she hit the top. And then when she moved here, she answered all your questions, told you everything she knew." I looked Tiffany in the eye. "It was important to her that you be happy and fulfilled. She loved you like a daughter."

"But what I need, Rue, is a job!" Tiffany looked almost desperate as she stuffed a croquette in her mouth.

"But how could she give you that?" I asked. "Lillian

wasn't hiring. She was doing alterations at the Clean and Bright!" I put the shrimp bite in my mouth.

"But what she *could* give me was an introduction." Tiffany gripped the table's edge. "All I need, Rue, is a chance to get my sketches in front of a decision-maker at a brand that matters, like Versace or Chanel."

I almost spit out my shrimp—because, oh, those sketches.

Suddenly, the young woman across from me seemed fragile, and I longed to protect her. She would surely be humiliated if she ever managed to get her work in front of some power player with exacting standards and no time to mince words.

"There was really nothing Lillian could have done," I said. "The people that you want to meet are all in New York." And Paris, I suppose. Milan? They weren't in Massachusetts; that I knew for sure.

Of course, I understood that Lillian could have sent a letter. She could have made a call, but I was almost sure she'd seen some of those sketches, and just...*whoa*. Any phone call would be wasted, as Lillian surely knew.

"Lillian didn't get it." Tiffany directed her gaze to the window, and her eyes grew hard. "She got to have it all: the experiences, the contacts, the feel of those fine fabrics in her hands." A tear rolled down her cheek. "Why could she not share?"

"Because she had a new life here." I reached out to touch her hand. "Those weren't really people she talked to anymore."

"Are you even kidding me?" Tiffany's mouth hung open. "Surely you remember who waltzed into the Clean and Bright one day. And did she even bother to arrange an introduction, show him some of my work?"

Oh, yes, I remembered. It was Pierre Blanchet, designer to the stars and Lillian's former boss.

About four months before, he'd stopped in to see her on his way to vacation in Cape Cod. News had quickly spread by way of those who'd been picking up their suits or tablecloths when the flamboyant Blanchet swept into the business with his entourage.

No way could Lillian have allowed Tiffany to show those sketches to a man who dressed A-listers for the Oscars. I winced at the thought of Pierre Blanchet peering down at one particular black and white atrocity Tiffany had sketched. The wearer would appear to be bound for prison instead of a premiere.

"I could not believe it when I heard he was here." Tiffany's hands were shaking. "I asked Lillian, 'What the heck?' and she just said he was busy." Tiffany sat back in her chair and frowned. "Well, he had enough time, from what I understand, to have lunch with Lillian at the Fisherman's Delight. And did she invite me? No! This was my dream on the line, and did she even care? Apparently, she didn't."

"Oh, of course she did." I reached out to squeeze her hand.

"I've tried to let it go." Tiffany wiped away a tear. "Because, well, she was Lillian, the one who was always there. Like, she spent the night at my apartment when I had that fever that just kept shooting up. And when I couldn't pay my rent this one time, Lillian wrote a check." Tiffany slowly spun her empty glass. "But then there are days when I see one of Blanchet's designs online, and it's just so fabulous, and there I am still sweeping hair off the floor at Reba's, and I…kind of lose it, Rue."

A chill ran through me at her words. How would that look exactly—Tiffany "losing it"?

"But it's okay," she said, making an effort to be calm. "Because I made a plan. Since my fashion dreams seem to be on hold, I've come up with a…project."

"What kind of project would that be?"

Tiffany hesitated. "I can't really talk about it. I'm really sorry, Rue."

We both grew quiet for a moment, and Tiffany's mind seemed to drift. "It's like Lillian had two sides," she said after a while, "and it wasn't only me who saw it." She stared down at the table. "Like there was this one time. That judge—Betsy Lawrence?—came into the shop to have Reba do her hair, and Lillian was there too. I took a break from Lillian's trim and ran over to the judge to hand her a drink underneath the dryer. There was this magazine that she had opened to a story, and I saw this list—the top-ten betrayals on TV. I kind of laughed about it, and I said to the judge that, yeah, some of those were brutal."

Tiffany scrunched her forehead as she thought back on the scene. "And the judge laughed too, but it was not a happy laugh, and she told me that real life was way worse than TV." Tiffany met my eyes. "I could clearly see her cut her eyes at Lillian when she said that. I could just tell, you know, that there was something there, something that was hurtful."

I leaned in a little closer. "Did she tell you more?"

"She seemed to be in a mood! She said I should keep my eye on my enemies, but that most of all, I should watch my so-called friends. And then she told me something that was super sad."

"What did she say?" I asked.

Tiffany paused to recall the words. "She said it was all because of a supposed friend that even things she loved—like apple blossoms in the spring—always made her cry."

I thought back to the note in its neat black cursive. *Wishing you bells and apple blossoms.*

It had been Betsy Lawrence that Lillian had been apologizing to eight days before her brutal murder.

Tiffany stuck her fork into a shrimp. "Like I said before, people think deep thoughts underneath the dryers."

CHAPTER TEN

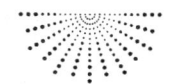

*T*he next morning a steady rain kept customers away, so I fixed myself some blueberry-favored tea and settled into the reading nook. Beasley wove around my ankles then finally found the perfect napping spot, his head resting on my toes.

"Bells," I mused out loud to Elizabeth. "Bells and apple blossoms."

She and I had been trading thoughts on how those two mostly delightful things could have broken up a friendship.

"One upstaged the other in a handbell choir?" tried Elizabeth.

No that wasn't it. I'd heard Lillian singing to herself as she roamed the bookstore aisles, and although I had loved her dearly, her talents weren't in music.

"One of them was jealous of the other's pink and white sweet-smelling yard?" I wondered.

That one did not work either. Lillian had never had an interest in her yard beyond keeping it trimmed and neat.

Something nonetheless had inspired a streak of vitriol in Betsy—and could have been the motive for the horror that had shocked our close-knit town. Or the motive could have been a stolen recipe for cupcakes. Or the exploded dreams of a would-be designer who had big hopes but no talent.

"If only I could figure out who was so furious with Lillian that night at the park," I said, pausing to take another sip. That threatening encounter could be a major hint about which unlikely suspect I should focus on—if I could only find a way to identify and check out these Believers.

If I found a connection among the Believers to Betsy, Ned, or Tiffany, that would be really telling. Or I might discover Lillian had been verbally accosted on that night by someone I didn't know. Then I would dig deeper to try to understand who else in her life might have held a grudge.

The boyfriend perhaps? Lillian had seemingly been murdered fairly soon after this man of mystery had come into her life. Why had she been insistent on keeping him a secret? Had she fallen in with someone with a dark streak that she hadn't seen? She could have been a victim of his temper or some secret from his past that brought violence to our town and caught her in its crosshairs.

Lillian had been smart, but romance has a way of blinding women to hard truths; most of us have been there at one time or another.

I took another sip of tea, contemplating more. Maybe I was wrong to assume it was one of the Believers who had argued with her in the park. Someone could have lured her there to harm her, a plan that had somehow failed, causing them to change course and go after her at work with that pair of scissors.

But something didn't fit when it came to that theory. The attack at the Clean and Bright did not seem to be the kind of thing that someone had pre-planned. The attacker, after all, hadn't brought a weapon; instead, he or she had gone after Lillian with her own pair of scissors. That made me think that someone had dropped by just to talk or pick up alterations, and that conversation had somehow turned deadly.

"I need to figure out who in town is a Believer," I said, half to myself.

Elizabeth picked up a stack of children's books she'd assembled from the shelves. "What do you think we should pick for next week's story hour?" she asked me as she flipped through the top book. "This one is a good one: *Can You Dance Like a Peacock?* That could get the children moving, which they love." She glanced at the stack. "Or *Baby Dragon's Big Sneeze* since it's pollen season."

There were a few factors that made for a good choice when it came to the picture book we chose for the weekly story hour. Humor and the opportunity for movement were both great. And if we could expand the theme to sell books to the grownups the children brought along, that was all the better. With the sneezing dragon, for example, we could put up signs to push our top-selling books on wellness.

A lot of bookstore owners didn't understand the marketing potential that could come with a children's story hour. Last month, the store had been packed for the reading of *Can I Be Your Dog?* A rescue group had been on hand with adoptable dogs, and Elizabeth had set up a beautiful display of adult fiction titles in which dogs played a major role.

With well-placed ads and the right signage, we could bring in specific groups who would likely have an interest in the chosen theme. That included many customers who might otherwise have never thought of themselves as readers. Who might we want to bring into the store next week?

Then I had an idea.

An image popped into my mind of an artfully illustrated cover. I'd sold the book last week to the mother of three boys, and she told me later they had loved it. I headed to the children's section, where I held up my selection: *Is that a Flying Saucer I See in the Sky?*

A slow grin spread across the face of my friend. "You're really serious about finding those Believers," she told me. "You are a smart one, Rue. Who knows? Your plan might just work."

"Well, I'm not super hopeful, but even if it doesn't, the kids will love the book. I'll put in some ads tomorrow," I told her as the plan came together in my mind. "In conjunction with the story hour, we'll announce a sale: something for all ages. The adults who bring their children in can get fifteen percent off any of our books on outer space."

"I'll get to working on the signs to go outside tomorrow," Elizabeth said with a nod.

"And I'll pull some books on astronomy, mysteries of the universe, and all of that good stuff." I set down my tea and stood, eager to get started on the project.

As the week progressed, things got busy at the store,

and I sometimes went for hours without thinking of the murder. Life in our downtown was inching back toward normal. There was less talk about the tragedy among the customers who came into the Seabreeze. Final plans for the community rummage sale ramped up, and life went on.

Andy seemed busier than ever, and I allowed myself to believe that was a good sign, that police were making progress. I did manage to get out of him that they had made no headway on finding a Believer.

"I do wish we could make some progress on that piece of the puzzle," he told me with a sigh during a rare call.

"Do you know any more about what was going on between Lillian and Betsy? Or is there any news on Tiffany or Ned?" I got all my questions out at once since he was so hard to catch. "And, Andy, I've been thinking about the boyfriend thing—"

"Rue, I don't have time to *talk* about that stuff. I need to *investigate*. In fact, I really need to rush off to a meeting with the forensics team," he said before hanging up.

Tiffany stopped by the next morning to present me with a brown butter toffee latte and buy a couple of romances. Her mood seemed improved from the last

A DONATION OF MURDER

time I had seen her. Shortly after that, Betsy breezed in from the courthouse for a copy of Riley Sager's latest book. I put on my best friendly smile for each of my friends, but I kind of kept my distance, using the excuse that the store was extra busy with customers that day.

Then I felt mortified about my treatment of my friends. This was Betsy. This was Tiffany. What was I even thinking?

Feeling like a bad friend, I slipped Betsy a free bookmark with a witty quote from *Pride and Prejudice*. After she read the quote, I was rewarded with a smile as she threw back her head and laughed, causing heads to turn. That was the kind of laugh she had—musical and infectious. Would a killer laugh like that?

I had no idea. I felt disloyal and suspicious and creeped out all at once.

Shortly after Betsy left with a happy wave, I looked up from shelving memoirs to find Ned standing next to me. For the love of Poe's raven! I took a calming breath. All three of them in one morning?

He let out a belly laugh when he saw me jump. "Didn't mean to startle you," he said. "The wife asked me to pick up the Prince Harry memoir, so here I am, and you are in luck! Today on the menu are the maple-bacon cupcakes, which I know are your favorites. I brought a peanut butter one for Elizabeth and a strawberry one for Dorie."

They were so kind and cheery, these suspects in the murder. Ned, in particular, was known for being generous, dropping into the downtown stores with surprise cupcakes for the staffs. In addition to his baking talents, he had an amazing memory for everybody's favorite flavors.

Of course, what *wasn't* generous, was stealing someone's carefully created recipe. But it was possible that Ned had never seen that little card in the antique cookbook. Perhaps he really thought the recipe was Kate's. Kate could have had the instructions memorized by the time she taught her grandson how to make the now famous cupcakes.

"Thank you," I said to Ned. I took the cupcake box, smiling at the orange bow tie and lime-green vest he wore. His choice of clothing tended to reflect the brightly colored, happy vibe that was a crucial part of his business branding.

Then I thought of Lillian's words underneath the dryer: about "garish colors" and some kind of "travesty." Had that last encounter between the two of them—the one that Ned was hiding—been a confrontation about the stolen recipe? Had Lillian somehow figured out the true origin of the key lime cupcake?

A DONATION OF MURDER

Now, Ned was staring at me with his eyebrow raised, and I realized I must have zoned out, lost in the spiral of my thoughts.

"Smile!" he told me, grinning. "You've just received a gift from the happiest spot in town!"

"Yes!" I swallowed hard. "That is really awesome, Ned. Now, let me help you find that book."

Our customers that week also included Ginger, Lillian's niece. The family had remained in town to clear her home after the memorial. Like her aunt, Ginger was a reader, and she had Lillian's easy smile and soft-spoken friendliness.

"We all loved your aunt," I told her as I rang up her pile of young adult speculative fiction. "She was a treasure in our town."

"This was her happy place, this bookstore," Ginger said. "She always wanted me to visit—your store and the beach, all the places that she loved." She blinked back a tear. "And now here I am, but there is no Aunt Lillian to show me all her places."

"Well, she mentioned you a lot," I assured her. "And she was very proud that you were out there busy, living your best life."

Soon it was the day of the story hour, and the shop was filled with eager children pasting hand-drawn aliens onto flying saucers made of paper plates. The store was fuller than I'd seen it in a while, and some of the adults were crowded around the display of books we'd called "Beyond the Earth: Our Amazing World."

Dorie was the reader for the day, holding up the book to display a picture of the aliens walking toward their saucer, suitcases in their hands. Even as the children waved their saucers in the air, bound for worlds unknown, they kept their eye on the book, caught up in the story. Dorie, a twenty-something-year-old ball of energy, read the book in such a way that even some of the adults turned their heads to listen.

Outside the children's area, the Seabreeze was filled with a steady hum as the large group of parents visited with one another and perused the adult selections. I was busily making my way from one group to another when I became aware of voices to my left.

A man in an expensive-looking suit shook his head and plunged his hands into his pockets as he spoke to a short older woman who was wearing large red glasses. "The closest star to us, you see, is trillions of miles away," he told her in a gravelly voice. "So you can understand that in real life, travel between planets is not as feasible as getting, say, from Boston to perhaps San Francisco or Atlanta to Seattle. One would need a time warp!" he said with a nervous laugh. "Which outside books and movies is not a form of technology that is available to us." He gave the woman a sheepish, apologetic grin as he pushed his wire-rimmed glasses off his nose.

The woman crossed her arms. "It's not available to those of us here on Earth," she said, "but who's to say that great minds on some of the other planets have not advanced their technology beyond our capabilities on Earth? Maybe one day we can ask them!" She raised a playful eyebrow. "You and I can't assume that earthlings are the smartest beings in this vast universe of ours. That would be a bit arrogant, don't you think?"

By then the kids had been dismissed and were milling around the crowd.

"Time warp!" screeched the parrot, startling the browsers.

The man let out a low chuckle. "Well, I work with telescopes a lot, and I haven't seen any of these visitors you speak of up there in the sky."

The woman shrugged. "Perhaps that is because they don't wish to be seen. Some extremely educated thinkers—at MIT, for instance—have begun doing work on the technology around the concept of cloaks of invisibility. Perhaps some even *smarter* beings—somewhere far beyond the Earth—began that research long ago."

She gave him a hard stare. "Which, sir, would explain why these visitors to Earth would not be visible to you."

Okay, I had done it. My crazy plan had worked and delivered to me a genuine UFO Believer, who might lead me to the person who'd argued violently with Lillian that day in the park. I listened in on the debate for a little longer, and I was fascinated. I really couldn't argue with anything the woman said—and her ideas were intriguing. I could sense the to-be-read pile beside my bed getting even larger with some of the very books I'd set aside for this event.

But for now, I had a job to do—for Lillian, for her family. The cops apparently weren't having any luck tracking down Believers. I could handle this part while they focused their attention elsewhere: on Betsy and that necklace or Ned and his big secret.

I held out my hand to the woman and introduced myself. "Such interesting ideas," I said. Then I lowered my voice. "From time to time," I told her, "people come into the store looking to find books about life beyond our planet. Honestly, these readers seem a little nervous about revealing to me what kind of books they want. I guess others in their lives give them a hard time about this little interest they've developed, and do you know what I wish?" I pretended to have just hit upon a thought. "I do wish there was a place all of you could gather to share your ideas."

"Oh, there are lots of us," she said, reaching into a massive leather purse and pulling out a small stack of cards, which she handed to me. "A lot of us believe we share our universe with others who may be as curious about us as we are about them." She gave me a smile. "It's a great big world out there, and we are not alone."

Quickly, I glanced down at the inscription on the card on the top of the stack. "Molly Kitchens, UFO Believers, Master Searcher."

"We are not alone!" cried Zeke, causing some gasps from the adults and cheers from the children.

"The bird speaks the truth," said Molly, her eyes boring into mine. "Meeting times and locations are listed on the back. Hand those out with care—to true believers only."

Of course, I would respect that. To true believers only, with an exception being made for a certain bookish sleuth on a quest for justice.

I winked at the Master Searcher. "You might just see me there," I said.

Then I caught Dorie watching, her mouth half open in surprise, the reading having ended.

As the Believer made her way back through the crowd, Dorie stared at me. "You really think that...?" She stumbled on her words, then her face broke out into a happy grin. "I've always liked you, Rue, but truly, honestly? You're way cooler than I thought."

Checking the card, I noted that the next Believers meeting would be held in just three days. Hopefully, it would bring me that much closer to finding out who had killed my friend.

CHAPTER ELEVEN

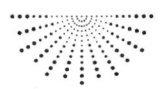

For most of the night, I lay awake as my mind bounced back and forth from one suspect to another. I decided to dig deeper—one suspect at a time. And I would start with Ned.

Had he knowingly for all these years been raking in the money with someone else's recipe? Or did he have no idea where Kate had learned to make those life-changing treats? (The cookbook that had held the card was old enough to have belonged to her, and who even knew if Ned or his wife had ever cracked it open.)

Of course, I couldn't simply ask him whether he had seen the written recipe for his signature dessert. If he'd been lying all these years—and maybe killed to keep the secret—no way was I asking the same question as victim number one.

Still, by the time I woke up and arrived, sleepily, at the store, I had an idea.

After a few hours, the steady flow of customers began to slow at last, and I reached behind the desk to get my purse. "Cupcake break!" I called to Dorie. "I will be right back."

"That would be amazing," Dorie gasped, and Gatsby's tail was a happy blur as he rushed to my side. Thank goodness he wasn't standing near that display of mugs.

"Did you know last night I had a *dream* about a key lime cupcake?" Dorie asked, looking up from a box she was unpacking.

At least one of us could sleep.

"Let me get some cash," she said, turning toward the back, but I waved the thought away.

"It's my treat," I said.

Gatsby was already racing toward the leash hanging by the door. Then he turned to me, barking happily, before running back to nudge my ankle with his nose.

"Well, I guess we need to hurry," I told Dorie with a laugh. "Gatsby seems to think he needs that Pup Cake *now.*"

Ten minutes later, I was standing at the bakery counter, studying with pretended interest the selections of the day. "Oh, the carrot-cake ones! I love those," I said to Ned. They were topped with little carrots he had formed with icing.

"An oldie but a goodie." He bent down with Gatsby's treat.

"My gran and I would always make a carrot cake to mark the first week of the summer," I told him. "I've tried once or twice to make it on my own, but would you believe I never even wrote down the recipe? So there's always something I can't quite remember. Half a teaspoon? Or a whole? And wasn't there something else I should be adding to this mix?" I laughed.

"Specifics are important," Ned said with a smile. "A written recipe can be the difference between disaster and divine."

I moved down the counter to see what other flavors were on offer. "Of course, I could call and ask, but it's kind of hard to catch her when I have a craving and she's in The Maldives or the Italian Riviera."

Ned glanced at the key-lime cupcakes, which were always front and center in the display of changing flavors. "For the longest time, I had to look back to the recipe my own grandmother used when she made these key-lime beauties. It was written on a card that I kept for years and years, and you should have seen that thing," he said with a chuckle. "There were ingredients crossed out and more of them added in. And there were little notes crammed in on the sides. Lots of experimenting on the way to perfect!"

There. I had my answer, and my chest went cold. If Ned had used that card "for years and years," there was no way he hadn't noticed the Fish House name across the top; he had absolutely known the recipe was stolen.

"Oh, but then, of course, I put that little card away a long time ago," said Ned. "After turning out about a million of those cupcakes, I could make them in my sleep."

Suddenly, everything around me looked so fake: Ned's smile, the neon colors, the oversized portrait of a happy Kate, supposedly a fearless, selfless nurse and baker extraordinaire, even though her obituary had skipped right over any mention of the war or her baking skills.

Had Lillian figured out the secret and confronted Ned when she picked up the cupcakes for the girls at Reba's the day before the murder? Whether he'd already known the recipe rightfully belonged to someone else, he'd still have a lot to lose if she told what she knew. But if he'd been pulling off a con over all the years, that said something to me about his character—and whether he might have progressed from fraud to killer.

"What can I box up for today for the ladies at the

Seabreeze?" Ned gleefully rubbed his hands together, his smile still in place.

My stomach was now churning too much for me to attempt to eat a cupcake. "Um, just a key lime cupcake, please, for me to take to Dorie." I forced myself to smile. "Got to watch the calories, you know!"

Later that afternoon Elizabeth came in, and she seemed out of sorts as she looked through a shoebox, lining up some vintage cards and photos at the edge of her desk.

"You okay?" I asked.

"Just one of those days," she said, pulling some old ticket stubs from a large envelope. "I had to cancel my reservations for next weekend in Vermont. Because my sister's sick."

"Oh man, I'm so sorry."

"Then I had the bright idea for something 'cheerful' to put up as a display. And what theme do I pick? *Romance!*" She pulled some dried petals from the envelope, sprinkled them along her desk, and laughed. "Why did I ever think that would cheer me up? Have you ever known me to be *less than despondent on* the subject of romance?"

I laughed. "At least we have the romance shelves so we can have a peek at other people's happy endings."

"Well, at least it will look nice," said Elizabeth. "And it will give me a chance to showcase some of these vintage couple portraits that I've picked up at estate sales." She nodded toward some photos at the edge of her desk, then pointed to a card. "And look! I found an old dance card from the nineteen hundreds."

"Wow, Elizabeth. This is looking great."

"It's amazing what you find," she said. "Even old love letters get sold with these estates if you can believe it. Which is another thing, I guess, that has me all bummed out." She sighed. "Grandpa pours his heart out in all these pretty words to Grandma, and what do his descendants do? They sell all his letters to a stranger for a quarter."

Reaching back into the envelope, she pulled out a valentine with a lacy edge and a cartoon kitten. "Everything today is just so sad!" she said. "Take this envelope right here. It came in from Betsy when we were doing that promotion with the Glove and Garter." That earlier display had been a promotion for a romantic comedy at the local playhouse. Elizabeth had invited residents to contribute their own photos and souvenirs on the theme of romance.

My heart quickened just a little when she said Betsy's name, but this was about some past love and not about the murder.

A DONATION OF MURDER

"Betsy's contribution was a downer," said Elizabeth, showing me the cursive note written across the front of the envelope.

"This is from a lost love," the judge had written, "but aren't there more of those than any other kind?"

"This one who got away sure sounds like a keeper." Elizabeth handed me a thin sheet of paper she had added to the mementos on her desk. "He lays it on a little thick in what he wrote to her, but still..."

I slowly read the letter and stopped short at one phrase. Betsy was his "apple blossom," the former beau proclaimed. Then there came a sentence about the sound of Betsy's laugh. According to the letter writer, it was like "the tinkling of the most joyous crystal bells."

Wishing you bells and apple blossoms.

"This letter..." I said slowly. "Do you know more about it?"

"I have the envelope it came in." Giving me a bewildered look, she reached into the larger envelope to pull out a smaller one in a light blue color. In the upper left-hand corner was the name and return address: the love letter had been sent by Elijah Masterson of Schenectady, New York.

I had met Elijah, I realized with a start. He'd come into the store with his daughter Ginger. His family was in town to mourn his sister, Lillian.

Which meant the relationship between Betsy and Lillian was much older than I'd known. Was this old romance connected to the animosity that Betsy had come to harbor for the sister of her former love?

"Did she tell you more?" I asked Elizabeth. "About this Elijah?"

"Oh, yeah. In fact, she did." Elizabeth shot me a wry smile. "Apparently *your honor* had a wild side in her college days. Nothing all that bad. Like breaking in at some ice cream shop to throw an ice cream party at two a.m. for her friends. Not super scary stuff. In fact, she left some money to pay for the ice cream, and she cleaned up too." Elizabeth let out a laugh. "But apparently, this guy came from an uptight family who had a lot of money, and they were putting pressure on him to do everything just right. Get into the best schools, land a primo job in finance like his father—"

"Date the perfect girl with the perfect manners."

"Betsy said the guy would not have buckled under pressure from his mom and dad, but he listened to his sister. And it was the sister who convinced him he should break it off. Which was just too bad. Because I got the idea she really liked this guy."

At some point, after working happily with Lillian at community events, Betsy must have figured out the unfortunate connection: she and her ex's sister had moved to the same town and struck up a friendship—which Betsy promptly ended once she understood who Lillian was.

Still, that hardly seemed to be a motive for a murder. Unless there was more. Was there some darker stuff in Betsy's past that Elijah could have known and passed on to his sister? The things she'd revealed to Elizabeth hardly seemed to justify an all-out push by his family to break up the pair. Were there other things that Betsy, for the sake of her career, couldn't risk the public finding out?

"Rue, you're turning white," said Elizabeth. "It's sad, but it's okay. This is way in Betsy's past."

"I'm okay," I said. "I just need some…water."

And for Andy to pick up.

CHAPTER TWELVE

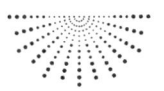

*A*fter that, I tried to concentrate on work. It helped that the store was busy with some major spring releases having just come out.

When I was not with customers, I started pulling cookbooks for a new display up front. This, it turned out, was a big week in Somerset Harbor for our local cooks. One of the bigger churches was about to host its yearly dessert social, and the Women's Club was planning a "Parade of Cookies," in which the public paid to vote for their favorite homemade treats to raise funds to feed the hungry. Competition among our local cooks could get pretty fierce, so I'd decided now would be the perfect time to showcase some of our gorgeous glossy cookbooks with cakes and cookies on the cover.

I was flipping through a book on Italian cookies

A DONATION OF MURDER

when I was joined by Pat from Fashion Flair next door. Pat, who must be nearing seventy by now, was a frequent customer in our cooking and travel sections.

"Ooh, this looks like the book for me," she said as she pulled out a newer title that featured recipes for desserts from New England inns. Then she lowered her voice. "Jeannie Albertson has taken the Parade of Cookies prize for two years in a row, but something from an upscale inn might be hard to beat. I mean, people pay a lot to stay in those kinds of places; they aren't just going to serve a mundane sugar cookie or your run-of-the-mill lemon bars in those upscale inns."

"I like your strategy," I told her with a wink.

"Okay, here we go—butter cookies filled with jam." She gazed down at a page that showed the cookies set out prettily on a Blue Willow plate. "This might just be the one."

With that, her older sister Alice padded down the aisle to peer through her thick glasses over her sister's shoulder.

"I really doubt The Almstead Inn would care if I 'borrowed' this one for the competition," Pat decided. "All for a good cause!"

"It's a recipe. Who cares?" said Alice with a shrug.

"Happens all the time," said Pat, who then turned to me. "Our Aunt Lou and our mother stole from each other all the time. Do you remember, Alice, that one Thanksgiving years ago?" She turned to me again. "Everybody raved about the three-cheese macaroni that was our mother's special dish. Then the next thing we knew, our Great Aunt Lou had spied the recipe lying on the counter, and what did she bring the next year?"

"*Four*-cheese macaroni!" the sisters said together, bursting into giggles.

"Oh, speaking of all that, you would not believe what I heard last month," whispered Alice. "The famous key-lime grandma—from the Cupcakery?" She paused dramatically, her eyes growing wide. "She was *Not. So. Good. At. Baking.*"

"Oh, go on with you," said Pat. "That cannot be right."

Alice looked around to make sure we were alone. But business, it would seem, had hit the first lull of the day. The only one around to hear was a tail-wagging Gatsby. He'd heard Pat mention cookies, I suppose, and was hoping she had some in her purse.

"Kate Lansing was a friend of my neighbor's grandma back when they were young and helpless in the kitchen." Alice pursed her lips. "Back in the day, young girls used to worry they'd never find a husband if they couldn't cook." She sidled closer to us. "So, this is what I heard. One day Kate was working—as a coat-check girl—and

A DONATION OF MURDER

she found several recipes in the pockets of a coat. And she just...well, she *took* them, and that is how she learned to make the few things in her limited repertoire. And all of that, of course, was before she gave up cooking altogether and turned to the drink," she added with a disapproving frown. "The recipes she took, came from The Fish House. Which, from what I understand, could really use the money those cupcakes are bringing in."

"And wait!" Pat stared at her sister. "She was checking coats? I thought she was a nurse."

"According to my neighbor," whispered Alice, "she dropped out of nursing school, was never in the war." She shrugged. "But I guess the nursing thing made for a better story—you know, for the press."

I swallowed hard as a really ugly story started falling into place. "And it was just last month you heard this?" I asked Alice. "Did you tell anybody?"

Alice scrunched her brow in thought. "I don't think so, dear. Although my memory isn't what it used to be." She paused. "Oh, on second thought, I did. When I picked up my dry cleaning a week or so ago, me and Lillian got to laughing about disasters in our kitchens, and I let her know that we were not alone. That even *the* Kate Lansing didn't know a measuring cup from a pasta strainer." She straightened her glasses. "Lillian was appalled, although I just thought the story was amusing—and a little weird."

I closed my eyes and took a breath, imagining the possible sequence of events. Earlier that day I had confirmed that Ned had known all along that the bulk of his business was built on a lie. And now here was proof that Lillian had found out about it not long before she died—just as I had suspected.

I pulled my phone from my pocket to check for messages, but there'd been no call back from Andy. Now I had even more to say.

"Ladies, enjoy your shopping," I said to Pat and Alice. "Please just let me know if I can be of help."

Moving toward my office, I tried once more to reach Andy before I burst with the news. News that pointed straight to Ned—but pointed straight to Betsy too.

CHAPTER THIRTEEN

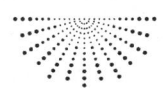

The next day, I was cleaning up the dishes in my kitchen after a hurried soup-and-salad dinner. The night before, I'd finally had the chance to tell Andy what I knew, and in our brief conversation, I sensed police were making progress and that an arrest was close. In his normal Andy fashion, he didn't say much more.

But now was not the time to mull over all of that. I had a Believers meeting coming up in half an hour, and hopefully, I'd spot a familiar face among those in attendance.

Whose face might it be?

I grabbed a raincoat from my closet. From the noise outside my window, I could tell the rain was already coming down. Just as it had done on the night of that other gathering of Believers when someone had been overheard berating Lillian.

I made sure the pets were set with their dinners, then I headed to my car and that month's designated meeting spot at the Somerset Harbor Recreation Center.

After a careful drive in the foggy early darkness, I arrived to find about ten cars or so scattered in the lot. As I got out of my car and opened my umbrella, I watched the figures hurrying inside, keeping an eye out for Ned's rotund shape or Betsy's determined walk.

Just ahead of me, a thin woman almost slipped after stepping in a puddle. Her face was hidden by a rain hood, and her ankles seemed to almost buckle in her stylish red rainboots as I rushed to take her arm.

"Whoopsie daisy! Thanks," she said in a familiar high-pitched voice. That was followed by a giggle. "Why does it have to rain at every meeting that we have?" she asked. "Are there forces in the sky who are hoping we'll give up? Who don't want us to receive the messages from those other worlds?"

Then she turned to me, and I gasped.

"Tiffany?" I asked.

"Rue?"

We stared at each other.

"I had no idea..." she sputtered. "Never in a million years would I have thought that *you* believed in..." She stopped, lost for words. Her eyelashes glistened with raindrops, although, thankfully, the downpour had stopped for now.

Could it really have been her who made those threats to Lillian that night in the park where the Believers had all gathered?

I tried to play it cool. "Oh, I'm not really sure what I do or don't believe about...all of that," I said. "But some of the ideas I've read make me want to find out more. It's interesting, you know?"

Then my young friend's eyes seemed to fill with a kind of desperation. "I *need* it to be true, that beings from up there have really come to Earth," she whispered. I thought I saw a tear trickle down her cheek, although it could have been some rain from a branch above our heads. "I need it to be true, because I need the money, and I need it bad," she said.

"But how could...creatures or whatever from Venus, Mars, or somewhere—solve your money problems for you? I don't understand," I said. I'd never heard that flying saucers came loaded down with cash.

And why had Lillian, of all people, been with Tiffany at that other meeting?

In my young friend's eyes, I saw a flash of something. It could have been despair or perhaps a loosening grasp on what was real and what was not. It was a look that frightened me.

"There's big money in this, Rue," she said, grasping my hand hard.

"In researching UFOs?"

"No, in *finding* them!"

"But..."

Her voice grew intent as she glanced toward the recreation building. "Some people in there, Rue, are absolutely certain that beings from beyond have been right here—in Somerset Harbor—within just the last few months." She eyed the sprawling complex, where an elderly man was holding the door open for his wife. "And there are huge rewards out there for finding aliens and documenting what you see. There are millionaires who have offered to pay fortunes," she continued breathlessly.

"But even if it's true and aliens exist, would they not be...well, almost impossible to find?" This was the worst plan for making money that I'd ever heard. And Tiffany had a job! She had a place to live. Why was she so desperate that she'd turn to this?

"Oh, well, sure. You're right," she said. "It's not an easy job to track down an alien." Now her hands were shaking. "Which is why I need to quit with my yammering and get myself on in there so I can take

A DONATION OF MURDER

some notes. These people are the real deal, not like those amateurs who are always thinking *Venus* is a UFO."

Tiffany rolled her eyes. "People do that all the time."

"And you need the money to—"

"I need to get to New York, and I need to spend my time honing my designs and trying to meet people in the industry. And while I'm doing that, I will, of course, need cash to live on. It's honestly absurd how much it costs to rent a tiny shoebox of a place in NYC." She looked me in the eye. "But I really need this, Rue. I need to make things happen for myself before I get too old."

"Tiffany, listen to me," I said as I took her arm. "You have decades left before anyone would ever think that you are old. Why don't the two of us get out of here and—"

"No!" Her eyes narrowed at me. "I need you on my side," she said, "just like I needed Lillian to support me with this new idea—which could change my life."

"Maybe together we could make a *new plan* to change your life," I said.

A plan involving reason and people who resided here on Earth. Perhaps earthlings with connections in a new and exciting job field that would distract my young friend from ever pulling out those sketches.

"Did Lillian ever tell you I brought her to a meeting?"

Tiffany asked me. "We came to one together, but she didn't understand."

"Well, I can't imagine this would really be her thing."

"But it was *my* thing, and all I wanted from her was to listen to the experts. And to give me a loan—which I would, of course, pay back."

"And it would be a loan to do exactly what?" I asked.

"To get one of those systems that comes with alarms and cameras. You know, at your front door? In case of a visitation!"

I winced.

"Then I would have some proof that aliens exist," Tiffany explained. "Some of those people in the meetings think there are lots of them *right here in town*. And that the visitors would naturally be drawn to those of us who believe."

"Oh, Tiffany." This conversation was growing more unhinged by the second.

"This one company that does security will give *a million dollars* to anyone whose cameras pick up footage that proves aliens exist." She paused for a moment. "Lillian didn't get it. She said it would never work." Tiffany wiped away a tear. "And I said things I regretted after that last meeting; I kind of lost my mind. But at least there was time for me to say I'm sorry before she...you know."

"I'm sure she understood. All she ever wanted was what was best for you," I said.

"We talked a few times after that, and one of those times, I hate to say, I was a jerk to her again. But what I'm really thankful for is the last time we had dinner. One of our traditions was to go out on Sundays to The Fish House, where Lillian and the owner were good friends. I think there are some problems in the owner's family—big hospital bills, I think—and she liked to buy me dinner there since business isn't great."

Now that was interesting. That would have given Lillian even more incentive to confront the man who was taking profits from her friend.

"I really hate to think about the things I said to her after that Believers meeting." Tiffany held back a sob. "And then the last time that I saw her—well, I lied about that, Rue." She looked me in the eye. "I was one of the 'mystery people' who went to her that last day to have alterations done."

"But why would you lie?" I asked.

"Because we fought again that day, and I knew it would look bad. The last words I ever said to my dear, dear friend—well, they were pretty rough."

I touched her shoulder gently. "There was no way you could have known that time would be the last."

"But, you know, I kind of did suspect it."

"What?"

"Deep inside, I had an idea we might be losing Lillian."

"You did?"

"She kind of gave me signs she might be leaving here." Tiffany bit her lip. "Things that made me think that when she left for France, she would not be coming back." She stared down at the pavement. "I didn't want that to be true, so I pushed the thought away. But so many of the things she told me in the end sounded like advice she wanted me to have if she was not around."

"Why would she not come back?" Had she put the trip together in a rush because she was scared someone here in town might hurt her?

"I have no idea why she'd want to leave." Tiffany crossed her arms against a sudden breeze and a misting of cold rain, which seemed to be starting up again. "But there were other signs. Like there was the time she brought this box of stuff over to my house. She claimed that it was just some junk that she no longer wanted, but I knew that wasn't right. Like, there was this statue that her husband bought her right before he died. And a little heart-shaped bottle of her best perfume. I just chalked it up to her being generous. But now I just don't know…"

"When was all of this?"

"She gave me the box one day not long before she

died. She'd come over with some stuff for me to mail while she was in France." A hand went to her mouth. "Oh, no. With everything that happened, I didn't mail her stuff."

If Lillian had been scared enough that she felt the need to leave the country, could she have written something down for the authorities to read once she was safe in France? That probably happened more in books or on *Dateline*, but it was worth a look.

"I'd love to see that mail," I said.

"Well, I probably should still get that stuff in the mail. And now, I really need to go. I'm late! And an expert is going to explain about high-powered telescopes. How to use them, where to find them, and what signs we should look for to help us in our search to prove we are not alone."

"This could be important, Tiffany—to help with Lillian's case."

She looked at me, confused. "But I don't see how."

"Just trust me on this one."

She thought for one second, then she nodded. "Well, if it's for Lillian, then let's go. I'll meet you at my place."

CHAPTER FOURTEEN

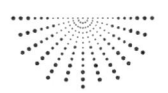

The answer, as it turned out, might have been there all along, in an envelope addressed neatly to police. There it lay among the jumble of makeup, fashion magazines, and chip bags scattered across Tiffany's coffee table.

"I had no idea," she whispered. "I never even looked. I just figured it was bills." And, admittedly, the envelope in question was buried in the middle of a stack of mostly routine mail.

We stared down at the envelope, which I was holding with a shaking hand.

Then fifteen minutes later, I was at Andy's door.

"Rue," he said, surprised. "Come on in, why don't you? I've been working late, and I need a break. I think we're getting close—*so* close—to making an arrest." He rubbed a hand across his scalp. "But, as usual with these things, there seems to be just one elusive piece we need to complete the puzzle."

"Which I might just have—right here in my purse," I said, reaching into my bag.

Andy took one look at the envelope and let out a slow breath. He moved quickly to his desk for a pair of rubber gloves. Then I huddled close to him as he cut the seal with a letter opener and pulled out a sheet of expensive stationery.

To whom it may concern. I now fear for my life after several threats during confrontations with Ned Lansing. All of this occurred after I discovered that the recipe for his famous key-lime cupcakes was stolen years ago from The Fish House restaurant in Yarmouth. Out of an abundance of caution, this information won't be reaching you till I am safely out of Somerset Harbor. Contact information is below if you'd like to know more. Lillian Louisa Clay.

Andy looked at me, a million questions in his eyes and I explained the series of events that had led Tiffany to remember she had Lillian's mail.

Things happened quickly after that. Ned was taken into custody that evening while the rest of Somerset Harbor was asleep or getting ready to turn in. Police announced the arrest in the next morning's paper, but very little information was released aside from the fact that the suspect had gone peacefully with the officers and made a full confession to the murder.

No one could believe it, and the lack of information meant rumors flying left and right as the businesses downtown filled up with customers the day after the arrest. Even the know-it-alls had nothing when it came to theories. Any way you looked at it, how could you connect a *murder* with German chocolate frosting, candy daisies, and uniforms and store décor so bright they almost hurt your eyes?

A little bit past two, Andy showed up at the Seabreeze with some food from Soups and Sauces, and he filled me in as we ate our late lunch in the back of the store. Ned had told police that to better brand his business, he'd created a fake past for Kate, including her service in the war and a love for baking. The real Kate, by contrast, had mostly made him sandwiches when he stayed with her as a child. But when Ned as a boy had developed a big interest in the culinary arts, she'd pulled out some old recipes from the back of a drawer. These were left over, she told him, from the brief time in her life when she tried—and failed—to become a decent cook.

She and the young Ned had not been able to believe how delicious the results were of their first cooking project. Friends and family had adored the key lime cupcakes and begged them to make more. Decades later Ned grew up, opened The Cupcakery, and knew right away which cupcake flavor he'd showcase in his store.

He was well aware that the recipe had come from a nearby restaurant. But, he'd insisted to the cops, he himself had done the hard work all these years of mixing up the batter and pulling the cupcakes from the oven time and time again. He'd promoted and advertised the cupcakes, and it was because of him they were now a tourist draw. So he didn't get the big deal when Lillian confronted him about what she'd learned.

He tried to talk her into keeping quiet for the sake of the town. The cupcakes brought in tourists, he reminded her, and everyone would lose if that were to stop. But Lillian Clay stood firm despite his arguments, his big smile, and his proffered gift of a box of cupcakes for his "favorite seamstress."

Andy said that Ned had wept when he confessed to making "stupid threats" to Lillian on more than one occasion and then losing all control on the day of the killing. After learning of her trip, he'd hoped to get things settled before she left the country. He'd gone into the Clean and Bright, hoping once again to persuade her to please keep his secret "for the good of everyone."

We were silent for a moment, knowing what came next.

"Does The Fish House know?" I asked.

"Not yet," Andy said. "There's still a lot of stuff on our to-do list at the station. Press conference coming soon."

"I still wonder about Betsy," I said thoughtfully, spooning up a bite of white bean soup. "Do you still not know how Betsy came to have the necklace? That has to mean something, right?"

"Oh! I didn't tell you." Andy dipped his bread into his chowder. "A few days ago, I got a call from William at the Clean and Bright. And they found Lillian's necklace! The thing had gotten shoved into the back of a drawer underneath the counter. Apparently, at some point in the day, the clasp had somehow broken. And that was why the necklace wasn't on the body."

"So, you are telling me that Betsy had *another necklace* that looked exactly like it? And that Betsy chose to give that same necklace away just days after the murder? What are we missing, Andy? You're always telling me that investigators should assume there are no coincidences in the world of crime," I said.

"Maybe not," he said. "But the world is full of things that we'll never know." He shrugged. "What's important here is that we know who killed Lillian and that man is locked away."

"Thank goodness for that, Andy," I said, leaning back

against my seat. I'd slept well the night before, the hard rock of tension having loosened in my chest. But delving into Lillian's life had opened up some questions that still were hanging open, and things felt not quite complete.

"I respect the fact that Lillian didn't want the information to get out about who she was seeing," I told Andy. "But can you please just tell me that he was a nice guy, that he was good to Lillian." It was important to me to think there was some joy during Lillian's final weeks.

Andy thought a minute then gave me a sad smile. "He tried really hard to make her happy, Rue. They were a good match I would say."

My thoughts drifted then to what might happen next after the true origins of the cupcake recipe were revealed to the public. Hopefully, that would result in a windfall for The Fish House. I thought back to the sommelier who had so enjoyed a key lime cupcake as a boy before the recipe was seemingly lost forever.

One in particular that I still dream about after all these years.

"Andy," I said thoughtfully, "I have an idea. Are you free tonight for dinner? For a little celebration...at The Fish House perhaps?" For my plan to work, I would need to get my hands on a key lime cupcake. I wondered if one of the employees at The Cupcakery had opened up the store.

"Let's have dinner soon," said Andy, "but I think tonight I might just turn in early. Last night was really crazy, and there's still lots of work ahead."

Maybe I would see if Elizabeth was free to enjoy a plate of some good seafood and to hand off to Carl "a little something for our favorite sommelier, who gave us such good service."

"Take a bite," I'd tell him. And then I couldn't wait to see it slowly dawn on him that the taste was close...no, not only close. This was *the very taste* he remembered from that magical bite of cupcake bliss he'd had as a boy.

Those tiny moments in our lives of almost perfect joy are few. And I could have the privilege of handing one of those moments back to Carl, nestled in a cupcake wrapper and packed into a plain white box.

For now, I'd be very vague about the nameless bakery where I'd found his special treat. After the press conference, he—and everyone around him—would understand at last, and business at The Fish House would hopefully explode.

As I mulled that over, Andy seemed to be lost in some musings of his own. "Instead of going out, why don't you let me make you dinner?" he asked me as a slow smile spread across his face.

A DONATION OF MURDER

"Um, *what?*" I jokingly poked his arm. "Does this mean you've discovered there are little knobs that turn the stove on in your kitchen? That you've figured out the difference between a pasta strainer and a slotted spoon?"

He let out a chuckle. "Well, you're always telling me, 'Andy, have some fun! Andy, leave the office at a decent time. Go out and get a hobby.'" He paused to clear his throat. "So...you'll be pleased to know that your buddy Andy has been taking classes. And I've become a pizza master. And not just any pizza. We're talking gourmet stuff."

I stared at him, surprised. "That's amazing, Andy, but why did I not know?"

"Before I told anybody, I wanted to make sure I was not a hopeless cook. Then this case started up. Not a lot of time to chat!" He took a sip of water. "But before all of that, I was driving into Provincetown for classes. And if you can believe it, I can make a decent pizza! We are talking homemade dough, fresh ingredients, the works."

He smiled at me proudly, but something in his words had sparked a memory. Pizza...Provincetown. It was sounding so familiar.

Then I let out a gasp. "Andy! It was you! You were Lillian's secret man!" I studied him and smiled.

He blushed, keeping his eyes on his food. "Is there

141

any mystery that you *cannot* solve? How on earth, Rue, did you know?"

"Well, Lillian wouldn't give Tiffany a name, but she did let her know that the new man in her life had taken her to Provincetown—for a pizza-making class. Which she very much enjoyed."

He stared down into his chowder. "It was very new, this thing with me and her, and it was Lillian's preference that we keep it to ourselves till we saw how things progressed. You know how people like to talk."

"I won't say a word, but…Andy, I'm so glad. And also, I'm so sorry. Sorry for your loss."

"And I thank you, Rue. It was a loss for everyone."

Andy and Lillian as a couple. Now that I thought about it, it could have been really perfect, and the thought choked me up.

With the senseless act of one man in a few minutes of wild rage, so many possibilities had been erased forever. Ned's arrest, it turned out, did not feel like a win; I could only feel the emptiness, all the things that could have been.

CHAPTER FIFTEEN

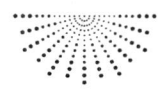

The next day, customers packed into the shops downtown with more than shopping on their minds. Everybody wanted to be certain they were caught up on everything there was to know.

I gave Ginger a sad wave as she came in with her dad and headed to our self-help aisle. They had a lot to process, I was sure. After a few minutes, Elijah settled into the Book Nook to peruse a stack of titles while his daughter browsed the new releases. Elijah, I noticed, was a handsome man with a little blond threaded through his thick gray hair. Several customers stopped to speak to him, and I felt a rush of pride over the way our town embraced guests as their own. The merchants guild had organized a "meal train" for Lillian's family, several of whom were still at the house going through her stuff.

In that same spirit of compassion, Beasley was soon settled across Elijah's feet for one of his daily naps. Although he was our shyest pet, he had an innate sense about who might need the comfort of a warm ball of fur pressed against their calves.

The store grew busier, and my morning was a blur of straightening books, working the front desk, and pointing customers toward the thriller, romance, or history shelves. I glanced again at Elijah, thinking I might ask him if he needed me to recommend more books. And it was at that moment I heard a familiar laugh as Betsy walked into the store and embraced a friend.

I saw Elijah look up, and in his eyes was a mix of softness and surprise as Betsy strode confidently toward the hot-tea stand, which was adjacent to the Book Nook.

As she reached for a mug, his mouth turned up in a smile. "Betsy. Betsy Lawrence," he said to her softly. "I'd know that laugh anywhere."

Betsy stopped, her arm frozen halfway to the tray of mugs. "Elijah," she said quietly. "I heard you were in town. I'm so sorry for your loss."

"It still seems just unreal." He frowned and then

A DONATION OF MURDER

looked up to study her some more. "Do you live here in town?" The soft smile returned. "What are the chances, Betsy? And did you know my sister?"

Betsy hesitated. "Is it okay if I sit?"

Wordlessly he nodded, and she took a seat.

"Yes, there was a time when the two of us were friends," she said. "We met volunteering. You know how it is. Small town and all of that."

"Imagine that," he said.

"I had no idea at first, of course, that Lillian was your sister. What with her married name and all." Betsy was quiet for a moment. "Eventually, though, we put two and two together." She paused and bit her lip. "I have to say, Elijah, I brought up the past, and I wasn't nice about it. I was pretty cold to her, I'm ashamed to say. And she even tried to reach out later and apologize for what happened way back then."

Very quietly, I moved to a shelf behind the Book Nook, where I busied myself with a little straightening project.

"She wrote me a nice note, but I was still awful to her. In fact, on the day she died, I walked to the Clean and Bright to try and talk to her some more about why I was so hurt. But I didn't do it; I just kept on going." Betsy stared down at the floor. "Now I wish I'd gone in and told her that it was okay."

Elijah leaned forward in his chair, clasping his hands between his knees. "She would be the first one to tell you to take it easy on yourself," Elijah told her gently. "All of that back then was my parents' doing. They knew I'd listen to my sister, so they used her, Betsy. They fed her a bunch of lies about you so she'd come over to their side. She came to have regrets. Especially when she saw that after you, I could never make things work—not with my first wife or my second." He gave her a soft smile. "I talked about you quite a lot. I told her about your laugh—like a peal of bells—and the perfume I always loved. And it became a code the two of us would use for simple, perfect things—*bells and apple blossoms.*"

She gave him a rueful smile. "So, I guess she no longer saw me as some wild hurricane, blown in to destroy her perfect brother's perfect life."

He let out a soft chuckle. "A big-hearted hurricane who smelled like apple blossoms."

He shook his head in disbelief. "Betsy. Betsy Lawrence. I can't believe you're here." He leaned back in his chair. "So, what happened after college? A husband and three children and a picket fence? Or is the infamous Betsy Lawrence still getting into trouble—the fun kind, of course?"

"No husband and no kids, and I've had to slow *way down* on the trouble. I will admit to you that this girl right here gets pulled into court a lot—but, guess what? I'm the judge! And getting into trouble is not such a good thing if I want to keep my job."

His eyes widened in surprise, then he let out a deep laugh. "Will wonders never cease?"

Betsy touched her neck. "I used to wear that necklace all the time, the one you gave me with the charms. I've lived a lot of life between now and then, but those were the days I always wanted to keep close."

"I forgot about that necklace. If I'm remembering correctly, I bought one for Lillian too. You both had birthdays in September."

"But about a year ago, I decided not to wear it. It was time, I thought, to let the past be the past."

He raised a playful eyebrow. "Until the past showed up in the Book Nook of your favorite store. Hey, I have an idea. Would you like to meet my daughter?"

I heard Elizabeth's voice coming from the next aisle. "I think Rue would know for sure the name of that author's latest book," she said. "Has anyone seen Rue?"

"I'm right here!" I called, stepping around the aisle to meet Elizabeth.

The day continued to be busy and at one point I noticed Tiffany making her way slowly down the travel-section aisle.

"Taking off somewhere?" I asked her teasingly.

"I think I might," she said, staring at the titles, then she grabbed my hand. "Rue, I just found out that Lillian left me money," she said in a hushed voice. "It was all divided up between her nieces and her nephews—but she also included me."

"Because you were family."

"She always made me feel that way." She smiled. "And that buys me some time, I guess, to figure out my life. I am truly over doing people's hair, because that's just not me. And, Rue, you were right. I've finally faced the fact that no visitor from Mars is going to just pop up out there on the sidewalks—or at my front door. My passion still is fashion, but I need a plan B. So…should I think about that plan while I am in Maui or Saint Lucia?" She slowly ran her finger across the spines of the books.

"I vote for Santorini."

"Great idea! I love it. Hey, that sale's coming up. Want to go together? Or I guess you might be tired of looking at that stuff. Since so much of it's been stuffed into the back of your store."

Elizabeth seemed to appear from nowhere and fixed me with a stare. "I think Rue has shopped enough," she said to Tiffany. "And she made a promise to herself to pare down her stuff. So that she'd at least have room in her walk-in closet to…you know, *walk in*."

Tiffany scrunched her brow. "I hear there were some killer purses in the stash that they've been sorting at the recreation center."

"It's a date," I said. "Good purses are essential—in all sizes and all colors." I turned to Elizabeth. "Closet space is overrated, and I can always line my purses up on a nice shelf in the guest room."

Elizabeth rolled her eyes, and I laughed at her expression.

Gatsby barked happily to greet a customer, and grief seemed to be slowly making room in our sun-kissed town for something more.

Some of life's perfect things had made a reappearance, like bells and apple blossoms and an exquisite taste from an old man's childhood.

"You never know," I mused out loud as Elizabeth headed to the counter, where a line had begun to form. "Someone might have put some really good antiques in their donation boxes."

Soon Elizabeth's head appeared around the corner of the travel aisle.

"You ladies let me know when you've made a plan," she said. "Don't you even think about going to that sale without me."

# # #

Thank you for reading! Want to help out?

Reviews are crucial for independent authors like me, so if you enjoyed my book, **please consider leaving a review today.**

Thank you!

Penny Brooke

ABOUT THE AUTHOR

Penny Brooke has been reading mysteries for as long as she can remember. When not penning her own stories, she enjoys spending time outdoors with her husband, crocheting, and cozying up with her pups and a good novel. To find out more about her books, visit www.pennybrooke.com

Made in the USA
Middletown, DE
20 June 2024